D0949481

Save Halloween!

Save Halloween!

Stephanie S. Tolan

Morrow Junior Books   New York

With thanks to
Robert Coles, whose book
The Spiritual Life of Children
shows the importance
of large thoughts
to small people

Printed in the United States of America.
1 2 3 4 5 6 7 8 9 10

Library of Congress Cataloging-in-Publication Data
Tolan, Stephanie S.   Save Halloween! / Stephanie S. Tolan.   p. cm.
Summary: Eleven-year-old Johnna, who is deeply involved in the sixth grade
Halloween pageant although her family views it as a celebration of an un-Christian
holiday, decides that she must follow her own beliefs.
ISBN 0-688-12168-3
[1. Halloween—Fiction. 2. Christian life—Fiction. 3. Schools—Fiction. 4. Theater—Fiction.]
I. Title.   PZ7.T5735Sav   1993   [Fic]—dc20   93-10635   CIP   AC

For my father
Joseph Edward Stein
1909-1992
with love

Save Halloween!

Chapter One

Dad says You're part of every good thing that hap-
pens to us, so—thanks. I was worried when Mrs.
Teator said the Great Teator Sixth Grade Halloween
Project was going to be a pageant, because You know
how scared I get having to talk in front of people. If I
had to say lines on a stage, I'd just squeak, like
always. But then she asked me to write it! Me! I
could hardly believe it. At first I wasn't so happy that
Brian Stern was going to be working with me, but it
turns out he has a terrific imagination. The script
needs to be really good, so I hope You'll keep on being
part of it. We could use the help.

Some people might think I'm crazy for talking to Jesus,
but my mom says we should think of Him as our best
friend, and since I don't have any other best friend, I tell
Him the stuff that's important to me. And ask Him

questions, too. Of course, He doesn't answer. That can be very hard on a friendship, but I do my best to figure out what He might say and make do with that.

Talking to Jesus is not the same as praying. I pray, too. My dad's a minister, and my whole family prays a lot. But when I pray, it's God I pray to, and I kneel down and everything. I think of God as sort of grand and powerful and a little scary. I try to pray only about important things, like world peace.

I know God and Jesus are really the same, but they *feel* different. I mean, it's like Dad being a minister, the Reverend James J. Filkins, and also just my dad. I talk to him one way as his minister self and another way as his dad self. His dad self is a lot more comfortable. Jesus is like that for me. He was a baby once, and a child, so for me He's easier to talk to. It's like He understands what it's like to be a person.

It was the first week after school started when Mrs. Teator announced that our project was going to be a pageant. Clear from kindergarten on kids hope they're going to get to be in Mrs. Teator's sixth grade. They want to be sixth graders so they can be the oldest kids at Stephen Foster Elementary, but they want to be in Mrs. Teator's class because of the Great Teator Halloween Project. It's different every year, but it's always something for the whole town.

Last year it was a haunted house. Lots of people come,

even families from Robert Taft Elementary on the other side of town. Mrs. Teator's class charges money for it, and the money goes to UNICEF, the United Nations Children's Fund. Every class wants to have a better project than the class before. Mrs. Teator has been teaching at our school just about forever, and for the last twenty-five years she's been doing the Sixth Grade Halloween Project. Ours was going to be her Silver Anniversary project, so we wanted to earn more money for UNICEF than any other class ever.

I could hardly believe she'd asked me to write it. Nobody's ever asked me to do anything really important before. She gave me a book on how to write plays and said she thought I'd do a fine job. Brian said it was because I have a reputation for doing good research reports and the pageant involved a lot of research. Its subject was the history of Halloween. "I'd hate the research part," he said. "The writing, too, for that matter. She chose me because I'm an idea man. Either that or because I live so close to you."

At first I wished she'd chosen a girl for me to work with, because doing a job like that together could maybe make people really good friends. But she was probably right to choose Brian. I didn't think any of the girls in our class would have ideas as good as his. He can sort of *see* the way things should be.

Brian wanted me to do the research all by myself and

just tell him about it, but I said that wasn't fair. So he went to the library with me after school. He read some stuff and I read some stuff and then we compared what we'd found. It was pretty surprising. Halloween's a lot older and a lot more complicated than I thought.

By the time we were walking home, I had a spiral notebook full of notes and an idea for how we could start the play. I wanted to talk about it, but Brian wasn't listening. He's a really different sort of kid. He's small and skinny, but very—I guess you could call it intense. Right then he was intense about the Roman soldiers conquering the Celts. Those were the ancient people of Great Britain who started Halloween. As we walked, he was using a stick as a sword and fighting every tree and bush and fire hydrant. It was embarrassing. I hoped nobody was watching.

"Listen!" I said. "I know how the pageant could start. We could have a witch stirring a cauldron. She could say that she missed the good old days when she was a young witch and Halloween was different. Then the rest of it could be sort of a flashback, showing how it started and how it changed."

He whacked at a tree branch over our heads and knocked some leaves off. "Witches are too ordinary. That's as bad as Kyle wanting us to put Frankenstein in just so he can wear his Frankenstein costume. Or Lashonda wanting us to put in a graveyard and lots of ghosts and skeletons. Standard stuff."

"At least those all fit Halloween. Melissa wanted to wear her princess costume."

Brian imitated Melissa's voice: "And my tiara with real rhinestones." He swiped at a hedge with his stick.

Melissa and Nicole had come to sit by me at lunch. Melissa said I was a really good writer and she was sure I could fit a princess in. It was the first time I could remember Melissa Sue Gallagher ever talking to me except to make fun of my clothes—I wear mostly plain jumpers or skirts and blouses, never jeans—or my hair, which is always a single braid. Mother says it's vanity to worry about fashion as long as you're neat and clean. With the girls in my class, though, neat and clean don't get you very far.

Brian waved his sword at me, and I ducked. "What we need is lots of fighting. Blood and gore. Jerome and Kyle and Ethan'll love that. Do you think the druids really had human sacrifices at— What was the name of that festival?"

"Samhain."

"Right. Samhain, the Celtic god of death." Brian pronounced Celtic as if it started with an *s*.

"Celtic," I corrected him, "like with a *k*. The people were called the Celts."

"I thought it was like the basketball team."

"The book said a hard *c*."

"Whatever." Brian jabbed a fire hydrant. "I wonder if the priests, the whatdayacallems—druids—killed people first or if they just threw them on the fire and burned them alive."

Thinking about it made my stomach twitch. "The encyclopedia says we can't be sure about the human sacrifices. Nobody really knows what the druids did."

"It would make sense, though. Offer the god of death a few people so he won't come and take everybody. I bet they did burn people." He whacked at a tree trunk. "It's weird that they thought trees were sacred, isn't it?"

I looked up at the leaves. A few of them were starting to change color already. Starting to die, I thought. Death. My stomach twitched again. Trees looked different, somehow, after reading about druids. Bigger and older and definitely stranger. "A lot of that Celtic stuff was weird. Standing stones and all. Stonehenge. Sort of scary."

"Hey, I know!" Brian said. "Let's have a druid do the remembering. After all, it would have been a druid who was there for Samhain, not a witch."

I tried to imagine a druid on the stage. It didn't work. "We don't know what druids looked like. How would we make a costume?"

"He could wear a robe. Like a wizard. You know, like Gandalf or Merlin. He could be all pale and deathly."

I didn't know much about wizards, but I got the idea. "We could use white makeup, maybe, on his face—"

"No, no, no! I've got it!" Brian brandished his stick

over his head. "We make him this decaying corpse, see, with his druidy robe all dirty and ragged, like it's been rotting in a grave for thousands of years. He could be like that crypt-keeper guy on TV. Jerome could play the part—he could do a great ancient-druid voice."

"Jerome? Pale and deathly?"

"Makeup. We could do up his face all gross—with the kind of makeup they use in movies for special effects. Latex and fake blood and all that. Nobody would even be able to tell what color his real skin is. His face and hands could be rotted like his clothes, sort of falling off."

I thought about Katie, who had squealed when Lashonda even mentioned a graveyard. Wouldn't she love a rotting druid!

"Maybe that's what I should be for trick-or-treating this year," Brian said. "I could get one of those plastic skeleton hands and have it sticking out of my costume with latex skin hanging off it. People could put the candy right on that. Last year Mom was on a history kick, and she made me go as Johnny Appleseed. Talk about boring!"

"Yeah, boring." In case he was going to ask what I wore last year, I switched subjects. "How about this? The druid could say he's come back from the dead, the way the Celts thought people could do on the night of Samhain. He could say he's returned on that night every year since he died—the night that's now Halloween."

"Yeah! And he could complain about how different Halloween is from the way it was when it started. We could show Samhain first, with the bonfires and human sacrifices and all. And then we could have a big fight scene to show how the Roman legions came up from Italy into Great Britain and conquered the Celts—" Brian had a short fight with a stop sign.

"And then the Christians took over—"

"And then we could do Halloween in America. Terrific. That's three acts—Celts to Romans, Romans to Christians, then America. That would give us two intermissions for selling refreshments. If we worked it like the movies, we'd make more money on candy and popcorn and pop than from selling tickets."

I nodded. I've never once, in all my eleven years, been to the movies. But it isn't something I tell other kids.

"Okay now," Brian said. "Close your eyes and picture this. A stage in blue light, like moonlight. And a full moon. Gravestones—we have to give Lashonda her graveyard, after all. And off to one side a coffin. A wolf howls. Bats swoop above the stage. Maybe there's mist sort of swirling around the gravestones. Like you can make with dry ice. The coffin opens with a creaking sound and a rotting corpse comes out."

I could see it. A terrific beginning. "What does he say?" I asked, opening my eyes.

8

Brian stabbed a telephone pole. "That's your department. You'll think of something." He jabbed his stick into a belt loop on his jeans. "We should work after school tomorrow, I guess. Your house or mine?"

I could just see the two of us working on a Halloween pageant at our dining-room table, under Dad's nose. "Not my house." Then I had to come up with a reason. "My brothers would drive us crazy. Luke already had his Halloween Project, and he'd probably just love to sabotage ours." I wasn't sure that was true, of course, but it could have been. Luke's in eighth grade at the junior high and sort of competitive. He might think our pageant would be better than his class's Halloween fair. The twins are in ninth grade, but they didn't have Mrs. Teator for sixth, so they wouldn't care. Actually, they probably wouldn't even be there because of soccer practice. But Brian didn't know that.

"Okay," he said. "Tomorrow at my house. If my sister Sadie's a pest, we'll lock her in the garage."

We'd reached our house by now. Mostly I just think of it as home, but with Brian looking at it, I was sort of embarrassed. It's pretty small, and its white paint is peeling. Also, the front porch tilts a little. Next door is the Rock of Ages Community Church, which is just a concrete-block building with a cross on the roof. The signboard in front has Dad's name, and the times of the Sunday and Wednesday services. IN JESUS, it says under that, EVERYBODY IS SOMEBODY. JOIN US. On the other side of the church is the big vacant lot that we use for parking.

Brian wasn't paying much attention, though. "You write the first act the way you think it should go, and I'll think of some ideas, and then we'll compare." He pulled his stick out again and pretended to attack the church sign. "Decaying corpses and human sacrifices and battles with the Romans. This is going to make last year's haunted house look wimpy."

I watched him go, slashing at bushes and trees all the way to the corner. And the kids in our class think *I'm* weird! Then I walked up the driveway between the church and our house. Our old beat-up blue Buick wasn't there, so I knew Dad wasn't home. And since it wasn't five yet, Mom would still be in the church office. Great. I could get right to work. And I didn't have to talk to anybody about what I was doing.

Chapter Two

Okay, okay, I haven't told Mom and Dad about how big a part I have in the Halloween Project. In some ways it's really sort of mine. Mine and Brian's. There's plenty of time to tell them later. Luke collected tickets at the fair when he was in Mrs. Teator's class, so it isn't as if we can't be part of the project at all. Also, I bet when You were a kid You didn't tell Mary and Joseph every single thing. Dad thinks You probably weren't perfect back then, because You didn't know who You were yet. Just like regular people. Probably You just expected to be a plain carpenter when You grew up.

When I got home, I checked the lentil soup that was simmering on the stove, and then went into my room and shut the door. There's one good thing about being the only girl in the Filkins family. I have a room to myself.

Matthew, Mark, and Luke share the big room upstairs, and Mom and Dad have the smaller one. That makes me the only one in the family with a room of my own.

It used to be the mud room, a sort of porch right off the kitchen. It's teeny, and in the winter it isn't exactly warm. But there was a big, poofy down comforter left over after a rummage sale two years ago. Mom took it and covered it with pale-blue fabric and embroidered *Johnna* on it, all in violets. When I get under my comforter in the winter, it makes my bed the coziest place in the house.

The best thing about a room of my own is the privacy. That was going to be important for working on the pageant. I got all settled, with my pillow fluffed up behind me and the garlicky smell of the soup all around me, and opened my notebook. At the top of a blank page I wrote *The History of Halloween* in my very best handwriting. Then I wrote what Brian had described about the opening the way the book about playwriting said to write the stage directions. Then, when it was time for the druid to talk, I got stuck.

How could he tell the audience who and what he was? And how would somebody that old talk? This was harder than I'd thought it would be. I started thinking, instead, about what the history of Halloween had been for me.

The first I really knew about Halloween was in kindergarten. We were going to have a party and everybody was talking about the costumes they were going to wear. I wanted to go as a crayon. A red crayon. But when I told Mom so she could make my costume, she said I wasn't allowed to dress up. Not as a crayon, not as anything. If the party hadn't been on a regular school day, I wouldn't have been allowed to go to it at all.

I cried. As usual, Mom called Dad in to talk to me, and he said Halloween was all about devils and witches and other bad things, and so it wasn't the sort of holiday we could celebrate. I told him crayons weren't bad. I remember just exactly how I felt then. Disappointed. Sad. But mainly furious. I really wanted that costume.

Dad took me on his lap and said that it wasn't crayons or dressing up or *me* that was bad, just the idea of Halloween. He said that all the stuff about witches and devils and ghosts, even if people didn't *mean* it to, even if they thought it was all in fun, might help Satan bring evil into the world. So we didn't dress up and go trick-or-treating or make jack-o'-lanterns. We had a church service every Halloween instead, to work against any evil the holiday might bring out.

I told him the school's Halloween celebration was wonderful, not evil, and described just how our classroom looked, with the twisted orange-and-black crepe-paper streamers, the black cats and jack-o'-lanterns and spiders, the pretend web made of black yarn and the bats and the pumpkin I had cut out of orange construction paper all by myself. "And there's a funny old witch riding a broomstick right up over the blackboard," I told him. I thought that would do it, that would make him see how great Halloween was. I was only five.

It didn't, of course. "A witch!" he said, and his voice was so stern I started crying again. "Witches aren't funny, Johnna, they're evil. Always have been and always will be. It isn't a good idea to try to turn ancient evil into fun and games. The old symbols are more powerful than the people who use them know. They appeal to something very dark and very bad. Halloween is a dangerous time. You'll understand when you're older."

Well, I'm older now, and I *still* don't see what's so bad about Halloween, not the way it is in Bradyville. I can't see how kids in devil masks or pointy witch hats have anything to do with the real devil or with real witches, either, if there ever were such things. Halloween isn't about evil, it's about costumes and parties, bobbing for apples and carving pumpkins—fun! And it's fun I have always wanted to be part of. Even knowing about druids and human sacrifice and Samhain doesn't change my mind. None of that stuff has anything to do with Halloween anymore.

That first year, when Mom went over to the church, I sneaked into her closet and borrowed a pair of shoes and a scarf and the hat she sometimes wore for Sunday services.

I put them and Daisy Violet, my doll, in a paper bag. Then I hid them outside in the bushes so the next day I could get them and take them to school. I put the shoes and scarf and hat on in the girls' bathroom and went into the classroom carrying Daisy Violet, pretending I was a mommy.

It was the only mommy costume in the whole school, and I got a prize for originality in the costume parade. I never told anybody about the prize, but I still have it, an orange paper badge with black ribbons. It's in my bottom dresser drawer under the paper lining. Every year after that I figured out some kind of costume I could do by myself, but I never won a prize again.

I was so jealous of the other kids' costumes, I could hardly stand it. The worst year was the year Jamie Kunkle came as a stoplight with red and green and yellow lights that really lit up. That was the year Melissa came as Glinda, the Good Witch, in a pink dress that had about a million layers of some kind of shimmery material with glitter sprinkled all over them. And Kyle came as a hot dog in a bun. His mother had ordered his costume from a mail-order catalog.

The boys and I never get to go trick-or-treating, of course. All during trick-or-treating hours, we're in church at Dad's Halloween prayer service. Last year all the kids were talking about one house where there was a coffin on the front porch. When kids came up the steps, the coffin would creak open and a body would sit up suddenly from inside, holding out candy bars. Half the kids were so scared they ran away without taking the candy. I bet I'd have been brave enough to get mine.

A knock on my door interrupted my thoughts. "Johnna, I need you to make some corn bread to go with the soup for dinner," Mom said. "I have some things to finish up at the church."

"Can't one of the boys do it? I'm working on a school project."

"They're all busy. And after dinner they have rehearsal for tomorrow's service. Remember, the Lord loves—"

"—a willing heart." I said the words as Mom did. A minute later I heard the back door close. Whenever there's something to be done around the house, the boys are *always* busy.

Matthew and Mark are both going to be preachers, of course, and Dad says they'll be very good. They always have some big part in Dad's services. Sometimes he even lets them do the Wednesday night sermon. They write it together and each give half. The sermons aren't as good as his yet, but both of them sound exactly like Dad. They look like him too, sort of, with his brown hair and chunky build.

Luke, who's taller and thinner and has much lighter

hair, is supposed to be a preacher too, but Dad doesn't have him do as much at church as the twins. He doesn't have as willing a heart about that stuff as they do. Dad has never asked him to do a sermon. My birth wrecked Mom's and Dad's plan to have four boys and raise four preachers, but I think Luke would have wrecked it anyway. He told me one time he thinks a preacher's life is boring and he wants to be a pilot. I don't think he's ever told Mom and Dad that, but he talks about traveling all the time, getting out of Bradyville and seeing the world. And he's always building model planes.

Still, if there's something to be done for church and Matthew and Mark aren't around, Dad asks Luke. And when Luke does it, he always tries to do it better than the twins would. Dad never asks me to do church stuff. I'm the mistake, Johnna Josephine, who was supposed to be John Joseph. Sometimes I talk to Jesus about that.

Like I said, He doesn't answer. But I figure God doesn't make mistakes, so there's some reason I'm who I am instead of who Mom and Dad expected me to be. I just haven't found out what it is yet.

As I was taking the corn bread out of the oven about an hour later, thinking very hard about what the druid should say, Dad came through the back door.

"What is that delicious smell?" he asked, and let the screen door slam shut behind him. He was wearing work pants and an old sweatshirt and carrying a manila folder stuffed with papers. James J. Filkins doesn't look much like a preacher. Even on Sundays, even in his best dark-blue suit, if he came down from the pulpit, he would blend in with the congregation and just sort of disappear. His face is nice, but kind of plain, and his hair's getting thin on top. He's not fat, but he's not skinny, either. Solid would be a good word. He dropped his folder onto the table and sniffed.

"Corn bread," I said, and held out the pan.

He sniffed again. "And do I detect lentil soup?" He went over to the stove and took the lid off the soup pot. "Yes." He stirred it with the wooden spoon, then tasted it.

"You know Mom hates it when you do that."

"I can't resist. I have a passion for lentil soup. Did you know that Esau actually sold his birthright to his brother Jacob for a pot of lentils?"

Did I know? Dad tells the story of Jacob and Esau every time we have lentil soup, which is just about every week. I'm not sure what a birthright is, but if it's all that valuable, Esau must have been starving.

"What a day!" Dad said, and flopped down on his chair. "What a glorious day this has been."

"What happened?"

"We live in the greatest country in the world. It is full of generous, caring people."

Dad says this a lot too. Mom says people are more generous when he gets finished with them than they ever meant to be.

"You know the Gephardts, the family whose house burned down last week—"

Of course I knew. The Gephardts were the main thing anybody had talked about around our house ever since. Dad had suggested having the Gephardts—all eight of them—move in with us. We'd been saved in the nick of time by the Red Cross. I nodded.

"Well, I found a used trailer for them this morning. It was owned by a woman who is moving to Arizona to live with her daughter. Her asking price was just about what the trailer was worth, which was three hundred dollars more than I had. But when she heard the Gephardts' story, she brought the price down three hundred and fifty dollars. So I not only had enough to buy the trailer, I had extra to get them a few more clothes from the thrift shop."

When Dad smiles, anybody within about a block has to smile too. I did. "That's great."

"And this afternoon the zoning board agreed to let us put that trailer on the Gephardts' lot while they rebuild. Not seven days since the fire, and they'll have their own place to move into tomorrow, if I can find someone to drag the trailer over. Praise the Lord. Luke!" He pushed himself up from the table and went through the swinging door into the dining room, where Luke was working on a model airplane. "I'll need you—"

As soon as the door swung shut, I went back to thinking about what the druid would say. And I knew. It was as if just not thinking about it for a while had given me the idea. "Lo, I have returned every year on this night for three thousand years. You call it Halloween, but to me, as to every druid, it is Samhain—*the night the dead walk.*" Excellent beginning.

Chapter Three

I thought Brian was rich because his parents are lawyers, but he's not. Of course, he's not poor, either. His mother thinks it's impossible to be rich and socially responsible at the same time. Dad would agree. He says You told some rich man he should give all he had to the poor and follow You. But Mom says she hopes that man didn't have a family. She says not to forget that You also said the poor would always be with us. That's another reason I wish You could really talk to me, so You could explain confusing things in the Bible. Like money. It's like we need it, but we aren't supposed to want it very much.

Brian's house is only a couple of blocks from ours, but it's in a very different kind of neighborhood. All the houses there are big. The yards are big too, with lots of flower gardens. I guess I was expecting oriental rugs and fancy furniture and expensive artwork when Brian opened their leaded-glass front door. What I saw instead was books. Shelves and shelves of them, from the floor to the ceiling. There was furniture, too, of course, but it didn't seem to be anything special. It was hard to tell because every-thing—couches, chairs, tables—was covered with papers and clothes and stuff. And more books.

When we went in, Brian's mother called to us from behind a door that she was working and she hoped we wouldn't mind watching Sadie. Brian made a face. "There's a plate of goodies in the fridge," she added, sort of like a bribe.

"We can work in the family room," Brian told me, and we went into the kitchen, where there were more books and papers on all the counters.

The goodies turned out to be carrot sticks and cucumbers and broccoli with a bowl of dip. Brian dumped his backpack on the floor and carried the plate into the next room. The family room was a lot like the living room, except that instead of books it had video cassettes. "My dad's a film buff," Brian said.

There was a fireplace and big television with a VCR, and two leather lounge chairs. In one of them was a very little girl wearing a purple net tutu over a t-shirt. She was putting a dress on a Barbie doll. Her hair was short and dark, like Brian's, but curlier.

"Out, Sadie," Brian said, and put the vegetables down

on a table between the two chairs. "We've got work to do."

"Who's that?" Sadie asked, and pointed her Barbie doll at me.

"Johnna. Now go away."

"You want to play Barbie?"

I shook my head. "We really do have work to do."

"Okay," she said, and got up out of the chair. "I'll be very, very quiet." She took a carrot and flopped on the floor.

Brian just shrugged. I sat down and got out my notebook. "I'll read what I've got out loud, okay?"

"Sure."

"Goody, goody, a story," Sadie said. "I love stories."

I hadn't even gotten to page two when Sadie got up, took another carrot, and went out.

When I finished, Brian just sat there, munching on a piece of broccoli. "Well? What do you think?" I asked.

"It sounds exactly like one of your reports."

"So?"

"So it's not a report, it's a play. Where's the excitement? And it's about Halloween, for pete's sake. Where's the scary stuff? All you've got is talking."

I had stayed up till nearly eleven working on it, and I loved the old-fashioned way the druid talked. Sort of like the angels in the Bible.

"Action. I told you yesterday. We need sword fights

and blood and gore. Bonfires and sacrifices."

"The druid tells about all that."

"But the audience has to *see* it. A play is like a movie. Think pictures, not just words. Okay, now listen." He jumped up and started pacing as he talked. "It opens up just the way you said, and the druid can say that first speech. It's a good one. But then the lights go down on his side of the stage except for just a spotlight on his face, and come up on the other side. Reddish-orange light— the bonfires. People dancing around them and throwing on vegetables and bundles of wheat. They can say Samhain gave them a good harvest so they'd have enough food and wouldn't starve, and now they have to thank him by sharing some of the harvest with him.

"Then they can bring on the human sacrifices—all tied up. Struggling and yelling and crying. Maybe one of them can beg to be let go. And somebody else can say they can't do that because if they don't make sacrifices to Samhain, he might make winter last forever, and that would kill all of them."

Brian stopped and closed his eyes for a minute. "We need scary music there, kind of building up, like in *Jaws* when the shark is coming. Lots of screaming, too, as the tied-up people get shoved closer and closer to the fire. Orange flickery light and dancing and people dragging and pushing the sacrifices toward the fire. Can't you just picture it?"

I closed my eyes and tried. I saw the stage with the druid's face in the light on one side and people sort of silhouetted against firelight on the other. Then, suddenly, another image came into my mind. It was a huge, dark shape that towered over everything else. "Samhain!" I said.

Brian stopped pacing. "What?"

"Samhain, the god of death. We could actually bring him on. He'd have to be really huge. And all in black. Somebody on stilts or something—"

"Samhain. Yeah. Huge." Brian thought for a minute. "But not stilts. Wait a minute." Brian squeezed his eyes shut. "I've got it. We put Jamie Kunkle—he's the biggest kid in class—up on a ladder—a ladder with wheels, so it can move. And we cover it all with a gigantic black robe. Then when the people start talking about Samhain, this gigantic figure sort of glides down with its arms out and stands over the people dancing around the fires."

I could picture it. It just might work. "He should come down through mist."

"And that's when the music starts to build—as Samhain comes down and the mist swirls all around him."

"Then," I said, "when the sacrifices are all done, when the people are burned up and everything gets quiet, we could bring on ghosts, some of the dead that were supposed to come back that night—"

Brian nodded. "Yeah. Only not kids in ghost costumes.

We rig up some pieces of real filmy cloth on black thread, and somebody pulls them on up really high, so they look like whatchamacallits, wraiths."

"We need the mist again," I said. "The wraiths, and then the mist."

"And then the Roman soldiers start creeping in through the mist. And the druid says how the Romans invaded Europe and came all the way up to Great Britain and conquered the Celts. You could leave that part just the way you've already written it. Except that we show it happening."

"That lets you have your battle."

"And the first act can end with lots of dead Celts on the stage and the Romans celebrating their victory!"

"Hey! Who ate up all the carrots?" Sadie was standing there, holding the empty plate. We hadn't even noticed her come in.

"Nobody," Brian said, and made his voice all deep and scary. "They disappeared by magic."

"You're fibbing!" Sadie said. "And I'm gonna tell."

"Time to lock her in the garage," Brian whispered.

We got the whole first act figured out, and wrote some of the lines people would say. Then we talked about how the second act should work. That's the one where we have to show how the Romans celebrated their own harvest festival on the night of Samhain, sort of using the traditions everybody was already used to, and just changing it to fit their different gods. And then how Christianity spread all through the Roman Empire and the Christians substituted All Hallows' Eve (which means "all holy eve") and All Souls' Day for the old harvest festival. That way the Christians, too, kept a lot of what people already knew. Brian said it probably made converting people easier.

It was harder to figure out how to make that part dramatic, because even though the new Christian holidays were still about death, there weren't any battles or human sacrifices. By the time we gave up on act two and I went home, it was really late.

Wednesday nights are church nights, so dinner is always sort of rushed. Dad and the boys are thinking about the service, and Mom, who plays the organ, has to be over at the church early. Since I never have a part in the service, I'm the one who has to clean up the kitchen. Usually I have to help fix dinner, too, but by the time I got home, there was nothing left to do but set the table.

Mom was looking sort of frazzled and Luke was fixing the salad. He had a white scarf around his neck and was chopping up radishes as if he was mad at them.

"You're late!" Mom complained when I came back from putting my stuff in my room and started setting the table.

"School project," I said.

"Or maybe a boyfriend," Luke said, hacking at a

green onion. "Jase Bishman says he saw you with Brian Stern at the library yesterday."

"Boyfriend?" Mom said, raising her eyebrows. "Brian Stern?"

"It's just a research project we have to do together," I said. Dad and the twins came in then, and we had to hurry and get dinner on the table. So there really wasn't time to explain that the research was for the Halloween Project.

When Dad mentioned "this fine and nourishing dinner" during grace, I peeked at the big bowl of macaroni and cheese in the middle of the table. It was the second time that week we'd had macaroni and cheese, and while I suppose it's nourishing, I have real trouble thinking of it as *fine*. You can always tell money's getting to be a problem again when macaroni and cheese shows up on the table more than once a week. Then Dad thanked God for giving us bounty and good neighbors to share it with and Mom made a sound that might have been a cough but sounded more like she was choking. Dad cut the prayer shorter than usual.

When we started eating, Dad asked Luke about the scarf he was wearing. Luke said it was real silk and he'd found it at the thrift store. He'd bought it because he was just finishing a World War I airplane model. "Now I need to find a leather helmet."

"Yeah," Matthew said, "and you can look just like Snoopy."

Luke's smart about some things but not others. If he'd been paying attention to what we'd been eating lately, he might have left his scarf with his airplane, out of the way. Mom's blond and has very pale skin, but it was paler than usual, and she had dark circles under her eyes. Anybody could tell she'd been worrying a lot. Now she looked at Luke with her mouth squeezed shut so hard she seemed not to have any lips. "And where do you plan to get the money for such a thing?"

"Same place I get the money for the models. Washing cars."

"It seems to me that if you have the time and energy to earn money for so many extras, you might share a little more of it with the church. Things are very tight right now."

"He could always tithe," Matthew suggested. "You know, put ten percent of anything he spends on himself into the Sunday offering." He put on that extra-holy tone of voice that drives all of us—even Mark—crazy. "That's what I do."

Half a second later he jumped, and I was pretty sure Luke had kicked him under the table. It was too late, though. Dad decided that since times were tough, tithing was a good idea—for everybody. Lucky for me, I hardly ever spend any money on myself. Of course, I don't have any except my allowance, and we already have to give ten percent of that as soon as we get it.

Then Dad started talking about the Gephardts and the trailer that they'd gotten moved to their lot, and I got to thinking about the second act of the pageant and how we could show people "a-souling" on All Souls' Day, going from door to door to get money or treats as payment for saying prayers for the dead. I guess I sort of tuned out. Next thing I heard was Mom's voice, about two octaves higher than usual.

"It came from *where*?"

"The church bank account, of course. Where did you think?" Dad was smiling his most winning smile. "There wasn't time to go looking for someone to hand out that kind of money. Mrs. Scott had another person coming to look at the trailer that very afternoon."

Mom wasn't smiling. "But I *told* you. I said you must not write another check on the church account without speaking to me first! James Joseph Filkins, how could you? Every penny of that was already planned for. The electric company is threatening to turn off the electricity to the church building!"

"There's our own account—"

"Oh, of course! The account you overdrew twice last month. We just barely managed to keep the electricity on in the house!"

"Remember the loaves and the fishes," Dad said, and took another bite of his macaroni. "Think of the fallen sparrow and the lilies of the field—"

"The lilies of the field don't have four children and two mortgages and a church building to heat!"

"God will provide. He always does."

Mom sighed, and pushed at the hair that had come loose from her bun. "But does He always have to provide through *us*? The Red Cross is helping the Gephardts, James. They don't even belong to our church. They've never put so much as a dime in the collection plate."

"We are not called to help only our own. We are called to help those in need."

"I know that. But sometimes *we* are the ones in need." Mom's eyes glittered as if she were about to cry.

Dad waved a hand, including all of us. "Anna, we are blessed. Truly blessed. We have each other, and we've devoted our lives to serving God just as we'd planned to. He always makes it possible for us to go on."

"I know, James. It's just that I get so tired—"

"Let us not be weary in well doing." Dad looked expectantly around the table. Luke was looking at his hands in his lap. I stared at my cold peas. "Let us not be weary in well doing," he repeated.

Matthew and Mark looked at each other and grinned. "Galatians, six-nine," they said together.

How do they do that? I wondered.

Chapter Four

When we were working on the second act, Brian asked something I couldn't answer. I still can't. Why did Christians burn witches? I know there are different kinds of Christians and we don't all believe the same things. Even Mom and Dad don't always agree exactly. But Dad says the differences are only in the interpretation of Your teachings. You said we should love our neighbors, and forgive our enemies, and not cast the first stone. What's to interpret? I can't see how anybody could have thought You'd want them to do such a terrible thing.

I was going to ask Dad about burning witches, but I decided to wait. Things were sort of tense between him and Mom, and I didn't want to bother him with hard questions.

On Sunday the scripture Dad chose was "He that

giveth to the poor shall not lack." And his sermon was about how we shouldn't worry about tomorrow but should let tomorrow worry about itself. The trouble was, not many people turned up for Church. Luke said it was the warm, sunny weather. People were trying to get in one more summer weekend. So the collection plate didn't help the money situation much. And you could tell Mom was worrying a lot about tomorrow. And the day after. And the day after that. Even Dad gets a little jumpy when half the pews are empty.

I was glad to get to school Monday. Especially when Mrs. Teator canceled the regular language-arts class period to work on the pageant.

Mrs. Teator is old. Older than Mom and Dad, anyway. She's short—not much bigger than we are—and her hair is short too, and gray and curly. Lots of teachers wear pants or even jeans to school, but not Mrs. Teator. She wears suits and high heels, always. When she gets excited about something, she sort of bounces up and down on her toes. That's what she was doing when she held up the copies Brian's mother had made for us of the first act. All around her face her gray curls were bouncing too. "I'd expected to wait till Johnna and Brian had finished the whole pageant before doing a reading. But this first act is so good, I decided we should go ahead."

Brian gave me a thumbs-up sign. I gave him one back.

"There's a copy for everyone who has a speaking part, and the rest of you can just listen. If you don't get to speak in this act, don't worry. There will be two other acts, and we'll be sure that everybody who wants a speaking part will have one."

"Does everybody *have* to speak?" Nicole asked. "I'm afraid I'll forget my lines."

Mrs. Teator shook her head. "There's a little screaming. Think you could handle screaming? They have to be really bloodcurdling screams."

"Screaming?" Nicole grinned. "I guess so."

"Then you can be a human sacrifice. You can practice at recess if you promise to stay far away from the building. We don't want anybody calling 911."

She started passing out the scripts. "You'll see the part you're to play at the top of the first page." She brought one to me. "Johnna, how about you reading the stage directions, so everyone will be able to visualize the scene."

I swallowed around what suddenly felt like a tennis ball in my throat. My hands started to get cold, like they always do when I talk in front of the class.

"Speak up now, so everyone can hear. That's for all of you, by the way. I want you to *project*. Remember that when we do this you'll be up on the stage in the high-school auditorium. You'll be quite far from some of the audience." She put on the reading glasses she wears on a black cord around her neck. "Begin."

I didn't do very well at projecting at first, but by the time I got to the part about the druid climbing out of his coffin into the mist, my voice had settled down. Usually when I have to talk, I keep thinking about everybody looking at me, probably making fun of me in their minds. That gets me all choked up. But this time I got to imagining the stage and the mist and the druid, and after that I didn't think about me or the other kids either.

"All right, Jerome," Mrs. Teator said when I'd finished with the stage directions. "You're the druid, so you speak first. Remember, you're thousands of years old."

Everybody stayed quiet for the whole thing. Then, when I said, "End of act one," they started clapping.

"It's great!" Lashonda said. "Really gruesome."

"Did the druids really burn people alive?" Kyle asked. "Just toss 'em on the fire and roast 'em whole?"

"Eeew," Katie said. "It's disgusting!"

"How are we going to do that on stage? How do we make a fire look real?" Jerome asked.

"I've spoken to Ms. Cappelletti, the high-school drama coach. She says several members of the drama club are willing to help us with the technical details."

"No way!" Jerome said. "No fair letting anybody else in on our project till it's done! Nobody helped with the haunted house last year!" Some of the other kids agreed.

"This is a far more complicated project," Mrs. Teator said. "And only a few students will need to be involved. Remember, we're going to have a fully equipped modern theater to work with. They have all the technical facilities to bring Brian and Johnna's work to life just the way they've imagined it. Ms. Cappelletti tells me they have a smoke machine, so we'll even be able to have the mist. But we need someone who knows how to do it all."

"My mom can sew," Melissa said. "She can help make costumes."

"That brings us to the next order of business," Mrs. Teator said. She went to the board and wrote *Crew Assignments* at the top. "This project is going to take real teamwork. I'm going to make a list of the crews we'll need. Most of you will have to be on more than one because there's so much to do. You can volunteer for the crews you want, but as director I reserve the right to appoint people if we don't get enough volunteers for each one.

"First, though, one very important job needs to be filled. We need a stage manager. That's the person who keeps track of the whole production. The stage manager keeps things running on time, tells people where to be and when, gives cues—"

"The boss of everything," Jerome said.

"I'll do it!" "Me, let me!" Kyle and Ethan called out.

Mrs. Teator looked at them over the top of her reading glasses. "Thank you, boys, but I think I need to choose the person for this job. Courtney?" she said.

Courtney Stubbins is probably the only kid in the class who's quieter than me. When Mrs. Teator called her name, Courtney seemed to shrink into her seat, and her face turned bright red. She has carrot-colored hair, so that made her clash with herself.

"What the stage manager needs," Mrs. Teator said, "is organization. And Courtney is the most organized student in this class." Courtney seemed to get even redder. "So, what do you say? Will you be our stage manager?"

Courtney, still clashing, and still shrinking, nodded.

"Good. Now for the crews," Mrs. Teator said. She wrote COSTUMES, SETS, PROPS, MAKEUP, LIGHTS, SOUND, TICKETS, PUBLICITY, CONCESSIONS, and USHERS on the board. "Melissa, since your mother sews, how would you like to be head of costumes?"

The minute she heard "head," Melissa nodded. "Does that mean I get to decide what everybody wears?"

I could just imagine her finding a way to put herself in that princess costume of hers. Brian made a tiara out of his fingers, and I had to cover my mouth to keep from laughing out loud.

"I think costume design will be something of a collaboration," Mrs. Teator said. "We need to know what the authors were thinking and what the budget constraints will be. A couple of local businesses have agreed to cosponsor the production, but we won't have unlimited funds. Now, who would like to be in charge of the set?"

In a few minutes the heads of all the crews had been chosen, and everyone else was signed up except me and Brian. Mrs. Teator said we'd act as consultants to all the crews. Consultants. It sounded so impressive, I could hardly believe it was me she was talking about.

Then Mrs. Teator had Brian and me both stand up and take a bow. "With this kind of start, this just might be the very best Halloween Project in twenty-five years!"

The class cheered. I sat back down fast. That was a cheer for me, I thought. Us. Amazing.

By Thursday Brian and I had finished the second act. The first part was about the Roman harvest festival and then the Christians' creating All Souls' Day on November first and All Hallows' Eve the night before, the night that had been Samhain and the harvest festival. Brian was afraid it would be boring because we couldn't have battles, but it was scary. Just like on Samhain, the dead were supposed to come back on All Hallows' Eve—graves opened up and ghosts walked. We used the mist again, and skeletons and ghosts rising up from behind the gravestones.

We had people go "a-souling" the way I'd planned,

because in the third act we could say that was probably how trick-or-treating got started. The druid said that even in Christian times people were afraid on All Hallows' Eve. Christians believed evil spirits came out that night to capture the souls of the dead who'd been loosed from their graves and take them to the devil.

Then he told about some of the other ancient beliefs that didn't go away when Christianity took over. People still believed there were witches—people who made a pact with the devil and learned to cast spells. It was because of their connection with the devil that witches began to be connected with All Hallows' Eve along with ghosts and evil spirits.

Then came the part about the Christians burning witches. Brian said that even though it wasn't really about Halloween, it fit with what we said about Christians' still believing in witches, and we needed it to make the second act as gruesome and scary as the first. I sort of wished we could leave it out, because I didn't want to have to think about how Christians could burn anybody to death.

As awful a feeling as it gave me, though, I had to admit the scene we made about the witch burning was pretty good. The special effects were Brian's idea, but I liked the speech I'd written for the druid. "For a long time we druids thought All Hallows' Eve was not as exciting as Samhain. But the new people didn't lose all of our old customs."

The lights would go dim on the stage then, and the orange light of the fire would come up. Eerie music would play and we'd show just the silhouette of someone being burned. Lots of people would be standing around the fire, watching. "After several hundred years, Christians put people they believed to be witches into the fire." Here he laughed an evil laugh. "Just the way we druids used to burn our human sacrifices."

Then another silhouette would take the place of the burning person. A huge head, with horns. "Who watched over those burnings? Samhain? Or Devil?"

I was just rereading that part when Luke called me to dinner. Matthew and Mark were setting the table and Luke was pouring the milk. I couldn't believe it. Matthew and Mark setting the table! Mom set a tuna casserole on the table and waved me to my place. "You were working so hard, I didn't want to disturb you. Still that research project? What is it, history?"

"Sort of," I said. And then, even though the pageant really was history, that began to feel like a lie. "Actually, it's for Mrs. Teator's Halloween Project. You know," I added, before she could focus too much on the Halloween part, "the one that raises money for UNICEF?"

"Halloween?"

I nodded. "Her class does a project every year.

Remember? Luke's class did that Halloween fair. Well, this year's project is a play—a pageant."

"And you're doing the research?"

Before I could decide whether to say I was actually writing it too, Dad came through the swinging door from the dining room, waving an envelope in the air. "Guess who I got a letter from today!" he said.

"Publishers' Clearinghouse," Mom said.

"A mission that wants us all to come to South America," Luke said.

"T.T.!" Dad said, and sat down at his place. "I haven't heard from him since Christmas."

Uncle T.T., Dad's younger brother, the famous one. I'd only seen him a couple of times in my life—he lives clear down in Texas. But I remembered him. I remembered what Dad calls his "Texas-sized" voice. And his bright blue eyes. I remembered much more hair than Dad has, blond instead of light brown. And a white suit. Every time I'd ever seen him, he'd been wearing a white suit, with a white shirt and tie. Also white shoes.

"What's he up to?" Mom asked.

"What he's always up to. Traveling, preaching. He says he's been to fifteen churches since June and raised a lot of money for every one of them. Crowds like never before, he says." Dad's smile faded a little. I remembered the half-empty pews last Sunday. Even when they're grown-ups, it's probably hard for an older brother to be outdone by the younger one.

"The only thing new is that he's taking some time off. Six weeks. He says he wants to get away for a rest. It'll be his first vacation in five years."

Mom had been dishing casserole onto her plate. She stopped with the spoon in the air. Her face was lit up like a candle. "James!"

Dad looked up from the letter. "What?"

"Does he say where he's going for this vacation? What he's doing?"

"No. Just that he wants a rest."

"That's it, then! That's the sign I've been praying for!"

"T.T.'s letter?"

"Of course. His first vacation in five years. He can get away from Texas and come here! Do one of his fund-raising crusades for *us*!"

"You mean spend his vacation in Bradyville, Ohio?" Luke asked.

"Why not? He can have a nice midwestern fall. And some home cooking and a touch of family. The timing is perfect. He's free just now, just when we need him."

Uncle T.T. here? For six weeks? I couldn't imagine it. The longest he'd ever visited before was a day between churches.

"I don't know, Anna. I can't very well ask him to

come here and do for us the same thing he's been doing down there. What kind of a vacation would that be? He needs a rest."

"He can have all the rest he wants. We'd only need a couple of good nights of tent crusade. Anyway, you know T.T. After three days off he'll be champing at the bit, wanting to get back in the pulpit. He can't rest any more than you can say no to somebody who needs a handout."

Dad frowned. "T.T.'s crusades aren't the sort of thing we usually—"

"James, we *need* some help right now. And I am as sure as I can be that this is the sign I've been praying for. It's practically a miracle!"

"Come on, Dad, please!" Matthew said. "We've heard about Uncle T.T.'s preaching all our lives. But we've never heard him do it."

"Yeah!" Mark said. "Think how much we could learn."

"Ask him," Luke said.

"James, it isn't a coincidence that just when we need him, he has the time to come. It's God's will." Mom's cheeks were pink and her eyes practically sparkled. "Besides, he needs us as much as we need him. Why do you think he wrote you about this 'vacation' of his? He's probably hoping you'll ask him to come here. He has no home of his own. He spends his life living in motels or staying with strangers."

"All right," Dad said. "I'll give him a call right after dinner. But don't get your hopes up. By now he's probably changed his mind and booked those six weeks solid."

I hope not, I thought. I hope not.

Chapter Five

Brian thinks everything that's good is bad in some way too. Like two sides of a coin—there can't be heads without tails. When I gave Sadie my cinnamon doughnut one day to get her to leave us alone, I said it was a good thing I hadn't eaten it yet. Brian said it was also a bad thing because now I couldn't eat it. I think maybe it's just in how you look at things. What do You think? If every cloud has a silver lining, does that mean every silver lining has a cloud?

Uncle T.T. said he'd love to come, and right away I realized what was bad about *that* good thing. When somebody stays at our house, whether it's a runaway kid or a battered wife or a man who lost his job and got evicted, that somebody always gets my room. The same, of course, with Uncle T.T. Which meant that for six weeks—six whole weeks!—I'd be sleeping on the couch in the living room. No more privacy. And six weeks meant that Uncle T.T. would be with us till after the Halloween pageant.

I spent Saturday morning helping Mom and the Ladies' Bible Society at a rummage sale they were having in the church parking lot. It had rained all day Friday, so Mom said it was a sign God was with us that Saturday was sunny and warm. Mom had looked a whole lot better from the minute Dad got off the phone with Uncle T.T. Now, even though money wasn't exactly pouring into the sale's cash box, she was all smiles.

Dad and the boys and a bunch of men from the Men's Bible Society were over at the Gephardts', helping dig the foundation for their new house. After lunch, with everybody so busy and so happy, I got away to Brian's house to work on the third act without anybody even asking where I was going. No trouble at all.

It was the third act itself that gave us trouble. Even Brian couldn't figure out a way to make it exciting. It was all about Halloween in America, and how it had gotten away from its religious origins and was now mostly just fun for kids. Brian said the goriest thing we could show in this act was somebody digging out the seeds from a pumpkin.

In my notes I had stuff about how early in the twentieth century Halloween had been a night for kids to play pranks and mean tricks, but we couldn't figure out how to show anybody turning over outhouses on the stage. Kids still did things like spraying windows and other kids with shaving cream, or egging houses and cars, or smashing jack-o'-lanterns, but that was hard to show on stage, and even if it was mean, it wasn't very dramatic. It couldn't hold up in drama to battles and human sacrifices. We could show trick-or-treating, but how scary could it be to see kids dressed up in Halloween costumes?

I suggested a bit about people giving out apples with razor blades in them, but Brian said his mother had told him that never really happened. It was just a story that everybody thought was true because so many people told it. She called it an urban legend. Whenever anyone had tried to find real evidence, like the X rays hospitals or police departments were supposed to have taken, or a kid who'd been hurt biting into an apple, they couldn't. If it had really happened, she said, somebody *somewhere* would have found some proof.

Brian said a good horror movie started a little scary and got scarier. Our pageant went the other way. Finally we decided to take the problem to the rest of the class and see if anybody else had any ideas. Monday morning Mrs. Teator gave us language-arts period and Brian explained the problem.

Katie said she didn't see why we had to scare people

all the time. Jerome said that was the whole point of Halloween. Melissa said since the pageant was about the history of Halloween, it should be educational instead of scary, and Lashonda said Melissa just wanted to be sure she got to wear her princess costume, which wasn't scary at all. Melissa said everybody could wear their favorite costume in the trick-or-treating scenes, scary or not, and she was head of costumes, so she could decide.

Pretty soon everybody was arguing with everybody else, and Mrs. Teator had to go blink the lights to get everybody to be quiet. "How many of you really like Halloween?" she asked then. Every single hand went up. "So tell me what you like about it."

"Candy." "Costumes." "Trick-or-treating." "Parties."

Then she asked if on Valentine's Day we could have parties and wear costumes and go from house to house to get candy it would be the same as Halloween, and everybody agreed that it wouldn't.

"So what's the difference?"

Lots of kids answered, but Lashonda's voice was loudest. "Witches and ghosts and devils. The scary stuff. There's nothing scary about Valentine's Day."

I thought about this. Scary. Halloween was supposed to be scary. But who was really afraid of kids in costumes? And then I had an idea. I started to raise my hand and then put it down again. But Mrs. Teator had seen me. "Johnna?"

I cleared my throat, because I was getting that tennis-ball feeling again. "When Halloween—Samhain—started, people were scared about almost everything. They didn't know for sure if they'd live through the winter. They didn't even know for sure that winter would end and spring would come. We're not scared about things like that. But everybody's scared of something."

"Yeah," Kyle said. "Like getting zits."

"Like Freddy coming out of our nightmares with his slasher fingers," Brian said, and Katie squealed.

"Car accidents." "Tornadoes." "Getting kidnapped."

"Like getting AIDS," Nicole said.

At that everybody got quiet. After a minute Mrs. Teator asked me if I had finished what I wanted to say.

"I just had this idea that on Halloween people can make fun of being scared. I mean, everybody knows the ghosts are kids with sheets over their heads, the spiders and bats are rubber, and the coffin on somebody's porch isn't real. It's all pretend. So even if it's scary, it isn't *really* scary."

Katie shook her head. "*I* think it's really scary."

"But even if you get scared, you always know you're being scared of pretend things."

"Maybe we need to get all this into the play some-how," Mrs. Teator said. She wrote FEAR on the board. "All right, class. What do you think most people are afraid of, no matter how brave they are?" No one answered.

49

"Nicole, you mentioned AIDS. Why are people afraid of AIDS?"

"Because if you get it you'll die?"

"Coffins and ghosts," Mrs. Teator said.

"Samhain," I said. "The god of death."

"I know, I know!" Jamie Kunkle said, shoving himself partway up in his seat. "I know how to make the end scary. Bring Samhain back in."

"You just want a bigger part," Ethan said.

Brian pounded his fist on his desk. "That's it! We can have all the trick-or-treaters running around on stage with their bags full of candy, and lots of laughing. The audience can be thinking that it's all just fun and games now. And then eerie music starts and Samhain appears at the very back of the stage, sort of watching over it all. Someone could jump out at someone else and there could be a scream. The druid could say that even now, with all the differences, Halloween is still about fear. He could say something like what Johnna said, about people being afraid and needing to make fun of it—"

I had closed my eyes to see the scene. Dim light and trick-or-treaters, some of them with lighted jack-o'-lanterns. Samhain, just a big black shadow above it all, and the druid off at the side, talking about fear. I was surprised to hear my own voice over Brian's. "People in scary costumes—witches and monsters and vampires—come out into a spotlight one at a time, like people's different fears. I can write some lines about what they stand for. And last of all someone in a skeleton costume comes out, there's a big crash of scary music, and Samhain starts to move forward, with the mist swirling all around him again. Everybody else on stage freezes and Samhain comes into the light right behind the skeleton. Then the druid says, 'Samhain, the Celtic god of death, is long gone. No one believes in him anymore.'

"And then Samhain says, in a real loud, real scary voice, 'But death is still here.' And the druid says, 'And we are still afraid.'"

"Ooooh," Katie said, and covered her ears.

"I've got goosebumps," Melissa whispered.

Mrs. Teator nodded. "So do I."

"Great ending," Brian said. "Great ending!"

After that it wasn't too hard to finish the script. By the time I walked home from Brian's on Tuesday after school, it was all done. The handwritten script filled almost a whole spiral notebook—the longest thing I'd ever written. I jumped over a crack in the sidewalk and felt as if I could have jumped over the Grand Canyon as easy as that. As if I could fly.

It wasn't just finishing the pageant, though. Just about everything at school had changed. It wasn't just a few of the unpopular kids who sat with me at lunch anymore. Katie did now too. And Nicole. Even Melissa sometimes. Instead of teasing me, she was being nice. Sort of sick-sweet nice, but nice. On Monday Kyle and Ethan had cornered a fourth grader who'd run off with their ball. They were threatening to pull his pants down. I told them to let the kid alone. And they did. Just like that. They called him a couple of names, but they let him go.

Even at home something was different. When I was trying to get my room ready for Uncle T.T. and Mom called me to do the dishes, I asked Luke to do them for me, and he did. Luke and I have always gotten along okay—sometimes when we were little, it was the two of us against the twins—but still, I hadn't expected him to agree, especially because it meant he had to stop working on one of his models. Of course, before the pageant, I probably wouldn't have asked him.

I jumped another crack. If I'd had a stick in my hand, I might have started a swordfight with a tree.

When I turned the corner onto our street, I saw in the drive between the church and the house a long shiny white car. On the door there was a seal, painted in what looked like real gold. In the center of the seal was a cross. Above the cross it said, THE REVEREND T.T. FILKINS, and below that, VOICE OF THE LIVING WORD.

I stood still for a minute on the sidewalk, just staring at the car. I was almost afraid to go inside. Would Uncle

T.T. remember me? And what would he think of me? Before I had time to think about the answers, the front door of the house opened and Uncle T. T. himself came out, dressed in white jeans, a white sweatshirt, and white sneakers, his blond hair sort of flopping over his forehead, his eyes as blue as I'd remembered them.

"Johnna Josephine Filkins! The prettiest little niece in the western world."

I could feel my face getting hot. "Hi, Uncle T.T."

He came down the sidewalk with his arms open and gave me a big hug. "I want you to know that I'm deeply grateful to you, Johnna." Now I remembered his Texas accent, too. "I understand I've put you out of your *sanctum sanctorum*."

"My what?" I croaked.

"Your room."

My face got hotter. "That's okay, Uncle T.T. I'm glad to do it."

With his arm around me and the smell of some kind of spicy cologne in my nose, I really meant it. Right then I'd have given up my room for the rest of my life.

Dinner that night, which was supposed to have been cold tuna-macaroni salad and green beans, turned out to be pizza that Uncle T.T. ordered in. "My treat, this first meal together!" He got three large pizzas—one with pepperoni and mushrooms, one with sausage, and one with hamburger and onion—and they covered the whole top of the kitchen table. Pizza, and him all dressed in white! I wondered if he had clothes of any other color.

It was strange, I thought, looking at my uncle, who was leaning back in the chair that Dad usually sits in, that adding just one person to the table seemed to crowd us so much. It was as if Uncle T.T., who's a little taller but a lot thinner than Dad, was somehow much, much bigger. As if he took up more space, even breathed more air than one ordinary person.

"My secret," he was saying, to answer Mom's question about how he was so successful raising funds, "is no secret at all. Nothing miraculous. Just what James and I have known all our lives, just what Daddy taught us. That the Living Word reaches out to people. It isn't what I say, it's what Jesus says through me." He grinned. "He gives me the gift of choosing the most important message and shaping it to the time and place."

"What *is* the most important message?" Matthew asked. He was probably hoping to copy Uncle T.T. the next time Dad asked him and Mark to do a sermon. "There's a whole Bible full of them."

Uncle T.T. didn't answer at first. He looked around the table at all of us, his eyes boring into each one of us in turn, so that we all stopped, not chewing, not swallowing, hardly even breathing. He took a bite of pizza, chewed, and swallowed it. "The message I give in my crusades—" he said then, his voice so quiet it was hardly more than a whisper, "—the most important one, is always the same." Now his voice got louder and the kitchen seemed to get even smaller. "The devil is alive. He is here today, working his evil, undermining everything that is good!"

Now T.T.'s voice dropped to a whisper again. "Right now he is in this town. Perhaps in this very *house!*"

As he said the last word, he brought his hand down on the table so hard, the pizza boxes jumped. So did I. I swallowed and glanced around the room. I almost expected to catch sight of a pair of horns or a tail darting out of sight.

Suddenly the kitchen was filled with a great big rolling laugh. "You see how powerful that message is?" he said. "You already know it as well as I do, and still it gets to you."

"That's all? You just say the devil is alive?" Matthew asked.

"There's more to it than that, of course," Uncle T.T. said. "But that's the bare bones. It's hard for people to doubt it. They see the evidence every day—every night on the evening news."

"It doesn't seem to be enough to get people to give money, though," Luke said. "I mean, don't they want to get something in return? People give me money to wash their cars—but they want to see the cars clean when I'm done. They wouldn't just give me money for telling them their cars are dirty!"

Looking from Luke to Uncle T.T., I noticed that Luke's hair was almost exactly the same shade. I'd always thought Luke and I both got our blond hair from Mom, even though Luke's was darker. Uncle T.T. smiled. "This boy's as sharp as porcupine quills, James," he said.

Dad smiled back. For the first time they looked like brothers. "I know."

Luke grinned.

Matthew spoke up so fast, I figured he didn't like Luke getting so much attention. "The people who come to our church and listen to Dad preach and put money in the collection plate see where the money goes. There's the Youth Fellowship and the Bible societies and Dad's Outreach Program for the poor. But even so, they don't give very much. You come into a town and do a tent crusade and then leave again. How come when they hear you, they give a whole lot?"

"What your father does and what I do are two different things," Uncle T.T. said, "but they have the same goal—to get God's work done in the world. He's the meat and potatoes, I'm the pepperoni pizza." He held up a slice of pizza. "Both are good nutrition, but one's a little snappier. People can count on your father to be there every Sunday, giving them God's word, keeping them going day by day, doing a good deed here and another one there. I bring them a one-time crusade, excitement, a big, loud, flashy fight they can join right now. And a reason for joining."

I glanced over to see how Dad felt about being called meat and potatoes, but I couldn't tell. He was just watching Uncle T.T. with no expression on his face at all.

"First I give them an explanation for everything that's bothering them, all the bad things going on in the world today. Second, and this is the most important thing, I tell them they can fight back. After I show them the devil at work, I remind them that God is at work too. I tell them they can side with God or they can side with the devil, good or evil, one or the other. Simple as that. Most people want to choose the good.

"Part of that is giving money. They aren't really giving it to me, remember. They're giving it to a church, in this case your dad's. And that church is working steadily for God and against the devil. But they feel like they're joining a real crusade, enlisting in God's army, marching under the banner of Jesus."

Matthew and Mark were leaning forward as if they were about to enlist too. Luke was poking at a pizza crust, but he was listening just as hard.

"What I do is take that general message I just told you

about, the devil working in the world, and tie it to something people can see. Something specific, right there in their lives. I show them the devil doing something directly to them, something as real as their own dirty car, that they feel they just have to do something about."

"So what is the something specific that you're going to use here?" Mom asked.

"The same thing I've been using all across Texas. Halloween."

I choked. A piece of pepperoni got stuck in the back of my throat and it wasn't until Luke had banged on my back and nearly sent the rest of the bite of pizza out through my nose that I could breathe again. I had to blow my nose on a paper napkin. Maybe I hadn't heard right, I thought. "Halloween?" I asked. "Did you say Halloween?"

Uncle T.T. smiled and his teeth seemed to absolutely gleam. "That's what I said! Halloween—the devil's holiday."

Chapter Six

Uncle T.T. says he gets his message from You. I've been trying to figure out how that can be. I talk to You all the time, and in my whole life You've never talked back to me once. Not once. So how do You tell Uncle T.T. what to say? He says it's a gift. But what does that mean? He says You want him to say Halloween is the devil's holiday. Even when I'm practically sure what You'd think about something, I don't actually know. How does he?

It might have been his vacation, but Uncle T.T. wasn't resting. By the time I got my sheets and blankets folded up the next morning, he was already in the kitchen, dressed in white slacks and a white shirt with the sleeves rolled up. He was sitting at the kitchen table with a legal pad and a cup of coffee, talking to Mom while she, still in her robe, with her hair down instead of pulled back, stirred the oatmeal.

"Organization is essential to a successful crusade," he said as I started setting the table around him. "Organization and publicity. We need to stir up the whole town. Get people talking. Set Bradyville on its ear."

It was all I could do not to groan out loud. Set Bradyville on its ear? About Halloween?

"We'll use James's contacts with other ministers—statewide. A crusade is always bigger than any one community. Some publicity we'll have to pay for—newspaper ads, billboards, posters. I'll take care of that. But most of it'll be free. We can use call-in radio shows, public-service television, talk shows, letters to the editor. We'll need all the volunteers you can pull in."

Mom's face was lit up with enthusiasm. "We can start with the members of the Bible societies—"

By the time Dad and the boys had come to the table for breakfast, Uncle T.T. and Mom had talked about local church newsletters, memos in other church bulletins, fliers, and something called a telephone tree, where a few people call other people, and those people call others, and so on. While we ate, Dad and Mom and Uncle T.T. decided to run the crusade for three nights—Friday, Saturday, and Sunday—starting October eleventh, two and a half weeks away.

"That'll get the money in pretty quick and still give us time to get all of the arrangements made," Dad said.

"And enough time for the word to build," Uncle T.T. added. They talked about where to rent the tent and the folding chairs and what kinds of lighting and sound equipment we'd need. They talked about robes and security guards and parking. The details were different, but it sounded sort of like the way Mrs. Teator had organized the class for the pageant.

The twins almost forgot to eat, they were so busy watching Uncle T.T. Most people, when they're talking, you can just listen to. Not Uncle T.T. You have to watch him too, because he doesn't just use his voice. He uses his whole body, his hands and his face and especially his eyes. It's as if he's really excited about everything he says. He's like some kind of magnet. You can hardly look away.

On my way to school that morning I saw that Uncle T.T. had already changed the sign outside the church. Instead of Dad's name and the regular services, now it said TAKE ARMS AGAINST SATAN! JOIN T.T. FILKINS, THE VOICE OF THE LIVING WORD, TONIGHT AT 7 P.M.

It didn't mention Halloween, and nobody from school was likely to notice our sign anyway. But I kept hearing "turn Bradyville on its ear" over and over in my mind. Everybody was going to know about Uncle T.T. and the crusade soon enough. Then what? My oatmeal sat in my stomach like a brick. Then what?

All day at school things were normal. Normal in the

new way. Melissa sat with me at lunch to show me sketches for the Roman soldier costumes. They were great—brown sleeveless tops with strips sewn on at the waist sort of like a skirt. She said her mother had wanted to use fake leather, but it was too expensive, so they'd be made of felt instead. "Is that okay?" She was actually asking me! I said felt would be fine.

Brian and I had an argument about the pageant's title. He wanted to call it "Ghosts, Goblins, and Ghouls" so it would sound exciting, but I wanted to stick with "The History of Halloween" so people would know what it was about. Lashonda was designing the posters and programs. She wanted to use Brian's title so she could draw ghosts and goblins and ghouls all over, but she said she'd put "The History of Halloween" in small letters underneath. I figured that would work. Mrs. Teator agreed.

By the time we were ready to start the first real rehearsal, I'd practically forgotten about Uncle T.T. and the crusade. Everybody was excited to get started. Even kids who weren't in the first act, which was all we were going to work on, came to watch. We had to have rehearsal in the cafeteria because we couldn't use the high-school auditorium till after the fall band concert.

Mrs. Teator called it a "blocking" rehearsal. Blocking means where the actors go on the stage. You can't just have everybody standing and moving around any old way.

A play is sort of like a dance, she said, and everybody has to know their steps. The actors were supposed to write their blocking on their scripts so they could memorize it at the same time they memorized their lines.

Courtney and the set crew put masking tape on the floor to show how big the stage was and where the curtains would be, and where the gravestones and the druid's coffin and the Samhain bonfire and all that would be. By the time they were done, some of the kids who had come just to watch had left.

Mrs. Teator put Courtney at a little table with a big notebook she had shown her how to make for the script with a blank sheet after every page. It was called the "production book," and Courtney's job was to write down in it everybody's blocking and any light or sound cues we knew we were going to need.

Brian and I sat together, and I could hardly wait for the rehearsal to get started. The actors were going to be saying my words. The first read-through in class had been great. This, I was sure, was going to be even better.

It wasn't. It was awful! It's impossible to imagine blue light and mist and scary music in the cafeteria with masking tape on the orange linoleum and the janitor running a floor polisher outside in the hall. The kids were in their regular clothes, holding their scripts and trying to figure out which piece of masking tape stood for what. Jerome

Teazel in a Cleveland Browns t-shirt, gym shorts, and high tops did not look like an ancient druid. And everybody was reading the lines without even trying to put any feeling in them.

Besides that, Mrs. Teator stopped everybody after every line to talk about where they should go next or how they should stand, and to give Courtney time to write everything down. Meanwhile, everybody who was waiting to go on or had already finished sat around on the floor acting bored, or talking or bugging each other till Mrs. Teator shushed them.

By a quarter to four I wanted to go home and hide under my blue comforter. We were only part way through the first act and I didn't know why I'd ever liked it. It was slow and boring and stupid. From the look on Brian's face, I could tell he thought so too.

A few minutes later Mrs. Teator checked her watch and whispered to Courtney. Courtney blew a whistle she had on a string around her neck. "Attention, cast!" she said. "Let the director have your attention, please. That means you, Ethan Elsasser!"

It was the loudest voice and the most words anybody had ever heard from Courtney Stubbins. Ethan was so surprised, he stopped shoving Kyle and actually shut up.

"All right, class," Mrs. Teator said, "I don't want anybody to get discouraged about this rehearsal." I felt as if she'd been reading my mind. "Blocking rehearsals are always tedious—that means boring, Kyle—and difficult. But they're a necessity. Just hang in there and it will all be worth it. This is a *very* good play, and by the time we're ready to perform it, there won't be any doubts. Now I have just a few words to say before we finish for today."

There was a groan, which Mrs. Teator ignored. "For the sports fans among you, I want you to think of me as your coach." Most of the boys laughed. It was hard to imagine Mrs. Teator coaching a team. "Courtney is your assistant coach." That was even funnier. "I'm serious. What we are undertaking here is going to take teamwork. Class spirit. We are the sixth grade." She bounced a little on her toes. "I want to hear you say that. We are the sixth grade."

Everybody said it, but the sound was ragged and sort of embarrassed.

"What did you say? I didn't hear you!"

"We are the sixth grade!"

"Better. Once more, a little louder. Who are we?"

"We are the sixth grade!"

"Good." She pulled at the cuffs of the blouse that stuck out from under her jacket sleeves. "Most of you are about to work harder than you've ever worked in your lives, and I don't want shirking or excuses. Each one of you is going to have to depend on every other member of this class. If one of you goofs off it hurts everybody. If one of you fails to do what you've promised to do, either it won't get done or someone will have to do more than his or her fair share."

Kyle made a face at Ethan, and Ethan poked him. "Kyle and Ethan," Mrs. Teator said, "between now and Wednesday night, October thirtieth, you will put aside your differences and work together. That goes for everyone. We have a team goal, and that goal is a championship project! We want to do it brilliantly, *and* we want to raise as much money for UNICEF as we can. I'll expect every one of you to work toward our goal, our championship, both individually and as a team. Now, who are we?"

"We are the sixth grade!"

Mrs. Teator smiled, straightened her skirt, and picked up her canvas bag. "Excellent. You are dismissed."

On the way home Brian was telling me about an idea he'd had to videotape the performance and sell cassettes to everybody's families. I wasn't paying very close attention, because I kept thinking about what Mrs. Teator had said—if one of us didn't do what we'd promised, it would hurt everybody. The whole project.

Brian was talking about how much to charge for videotapes when I noticed the flier tacked to a telephone pole.

Uncle T.T's name and picture were in the middle. BANISH SATAN was printed across the top in big red letters, and across the bottom, STOP HALLOWEEN.

Chapter Seven

Mrs. Teator says the Halloween pageant is a team effort. That's what Mom says about the crusade. How can I be on both teams? I want to think I can because they're playing different games, but what if they're not? What if they're in the same game on opposite sides? Can I be me, Johnna the sixth grader, coauthor of the Halloween pageant, and me, Johnna Josephine Filkins, Christian, too? The way You're You, Jesus, and also You, God? And if I can't be both, what then?

Brian didn't notice the flier, and I made myself keep walking as if I hadn't noticed it either. The fliers didn't mention a time or place for the crusade meetings, so I figured Uncle T.T. had brought them with him from Texas. He probably used them in every town he went to—the first step to get people talking.

The next step was the regular Wednesday night prayer service. Uncle T.T. was giving the sermon instead of Dad. When I got home, Mom was at the church office calling people to let them know. She and some of the Women's Bible Society had been on the phone all afternoon. Matthew, Mark, and Luke were over in the sanctuary with Uncle T.T. and Dad planning the service.

So I was left to get dinner. I found myself talking to Jesus quite a lot while I fixed spaghetti and a salad. Even if He couldn't answer, I needed to feel like He was listening. On my side and listening.

All through dinner Dad and Uncle T.T. had a "discussion" about what scriptures Matthew and Mark ought to read at the service. Now they sounded like brothers. It was the kind of discussion that would have had Matthew and Luke kicking each other under the table. Every one Uncle T.T. wanted had the devil in it and every one Dad wanted was either about God or about love.

Then everybody went to get ready for the service and I was by myself again. I cleaned up the kitchen and changed into a clean navy-blue jumper. When I'd washed my face and rebraided my hair, I stared at myself in the mirror. Just one face. One very plain face with blond bangs and one braid and ears with no earring holes. Could that face be two different people?

When I went out the back door, I could hardly believe

my eyes. The parking lot was almost full and people were still arriving. On Wednesday night! Usually we figure we're a success if we get ten families.

Inside, I smiled at the people I knew, the church members who come to every service and the ones who come Sundays but hardly ever on Wednesdays, and I smiled at strangers—lots of strangers. Mom was at the piano playing "Amazing Grace," but there were so many people talking, they almost drowned her out.

I went down the center aisle to the front pew where I always sit. As usual, Mrs. Quigley was there. She's an old lady Mom says is so faithful because she's outlived all her family and friends and she needs company. As usual, she'd saved a seat for me. This was the first time, though, she'd ever really needed to.

"Some turnout. That uncle of yours has a reputation that brings 'em in."

Matthew and Mark were standing in front of the altar wearing their royal-blue robes. Their hair was slicked back, and their faces were practically shiny from scrubbing. Each of them held an open Bible. They looked like identical statues. Usually it's easy to tell them apart because Matthew talks about ten times as much as Mark. But you have to know them awfully well to see the differences when they're just standing.

I could see only Mom's back as she sat at the piano,

playing "Amazing Grace" over and over. But I could imagine how her face looked. If all these people gave money when we passed the collection plate, Uncle T.T.'s visit would already be working.

Dad, wearing his usual dark suit and tie, was on the bench behind the pulpit, and Luke, in his blue robe, was next to him. Luke usually wears his hair like the twins, all slicked back. But now it was falling over his forehead. Uncle T.T. was nowhere to be seen.

When everybody was finally in and sitting, Mom ended with a big double-chord "amen." The rustling and talking stopped and the church got quiet. Matthew took one step forward. "The reading we begin with this evening is from First Peter, chapter five, verse eight. 'Be sober, be vigilant; because your adversary the devil, as a roaring lion, walketh about, seeking whom he may devour.'"

Uncle T.T. must have won the discussion.

Then Matthew stepped back and Mark stepped forward. "My text is Romans, chapter eight, verse thirty-one. 'What shall we then say to these things? If God be for us, who can be against us?'"

Compromise. That one was Dad's.

I was thinking about the devil, and whether he really was alive in the world and really could devour people, and missed Dad's invocation and opening prayer. When I tuned in again, he was standing at the pulpit, well into his introduction.

". . . throughout the state of Texas, taking the Living Word to one community after another. By rights he deserves a rest. But this is a man who does not tire of doing the work of the Lord. In our church family we often call one another brother and sister to symbolize our kinship and the fatherhood of God Almighty. Tonight I'd like to introduce to you my brother in Jesus *and* my brother in the blood and bone—the Reverend T.T. Filkins, the Voice of the Living Word!"

The applause surprised me. Nobody had ever clapped during a prayer service before. Then, when Uncle T.T. didn't appear, there was a sort of shuffling. People, still clapping, started shifting around looking for him. Dad sat down next to Luke again.

Just when the applause died out and people started whispering, Uncle T.T.'s voice boomed from the back of the church. *"Violence! Pestilence! Death! Destruction! These are the works of Satan. These are the works of the devil alive in America today!"* When the words stopped, it felt as if they'd left echoes in the corners of the building. Then there was total silence, not even a cough, not even a child fidgeting. I turned around to look, and everybody else was doing the same, trying to see where the voice had come from. Suddenly Uncle T.T. was there in the aisle, striding forward in his white suit, white shirt and tie, white shoes.

As he came he spoke again, this time more quietly. You had to strain to hear. It was as if everyone was frozen, not moving, just listening. "Satan, I said, alive in Texas, in Denton and Dallas, in Houston and Odessa. Alive as well in Cleveland and Columbus and Bradyville, Ohio."

When he reached the front of the church, he turned and looked out at the crowd. "How many of you," he asked, "read a newspaper today?"

I could hear the sound of movement as people raised their hands behind me.

"Or heard the news on the radio or watched it on TV?"

More hands went up.

"And what did you find in the news?" There was a brief silence, as Uncle T.T. went up the steps and took his place behind the pulpit. "I'll tell you what you found there. You found war. You found starvation. You found pestilence. And these things are happening not only in the farthest corners of the world, they are happening right here in this fair land of ours, this Christian country we love so much. We live in perilous times. There is violence and there is hunger, there is every kind of perversion and every kind of addiction, there is greed and there is poverty."

He paused and stood looking out at the congregation. "And I don't mean that all these can be found only in our cities. They can be found just as surely right here in Bradyville, Ohio. How many of you locked your houses before coming here tonight?"

Mrs. Quigley put her hand up, and it sounded as if just about everyone else did too.

"Hardworking, God-fearing people like you must worry about whether your homes are safe, whether someone is going to come out of the shadows some night and mug you, whether someone is going to put a gun to your head and steal your car if you stop at a red light. There are drug dealers on the street corners even here. Ask your high-school sons and daughters if they know where to get drugs."

Not just high school, I thought. Ethan Elsasser had bragged clear back in fourth grade that he'd smoked marijuana and knew how to get other stuff. I wasn't sure he'd really done it back then, but I figured he knew how to get drugs if he wanted. And he wasn't the only one. I'd seen the kids from junior high who hung around the playground and outside the Dairy Mart.

I realized I'd missed what Uncle T.T. said next. I looked up. He was holding on to the edges of the pulpit, his hands still for a moment. "—cannot turn on your television set or pick up a magazine or go to a movie theater without being exposed to sex and violence and human degradation."

He paused then and just looked out over the congregation. "Am I right, brothers and sisters?" he shouted suddenly. "Do you recognize the world I describe to you?"

In our church people just sit and listen. They don't usually talk back. But this time they did. "Right, brother," and "Amen," and "Yes, sir!"

When the voices died out, Uncle T.T. stood for a moment. When he started talking again, he used what Mrs. Teator would have called a stage whisper. It sounded like a whisper but was so loud that it carried clear to the doors at the back. "This, my friends, is *chaos*. The work of Satan." He changed to his normal voice. "From the serpent in the garden to the drug dealer in the school playground, Satan has been abroad among us." He paused for a moment and then began again, a little louder. "And from the serpent in the garden until this very day, we ourselves have encouraged him. Each of you has opened your lives to Satan and invited him in. I tell you, you have invited him in!"

There was a sort of murmur through the audience. Mrs. Quigley shook her head. "Not I," she muttered.

"You think you have not helped Satan?" Uncle T.T. said, even louder. "You think you have been vigilant against him? Think again, I say to you, think again."

There was a shuffling of feet. Coughs. "A little less than five weeks from today Bradyville, along with towns and cities across this land, will open its doors and beg Satan to enter. In private homes, in shopping malls, in schools and on the streets, people will celebrate the devil's most sacred night. There will be fires, looting, vandalism, drunkenness, and violence."

"Halloween," I heard someone whisper. "He means Halloween."

"Halloween!" Uncle T.T. shouted almost at the same moment. "Satan's own holiday! Halloween—a celebration of evil begun in the shadowy darkness of a pagan time. A celebration of Satan, of death, witchcraft, and sorcery!" He stopped speaking. He raised his hands toward the people and looked upward. I couldn't help looking up too, as if there might be something above him other than the cracked ceiling.

After a moment he looked out at the people again. "I say that you have *not* been vigilant. Halloween is an abomination in the sight of God. It sends a message to Satan. It tells him that we welcome what he brings into the world. It tells him that we are on his side."

There was a stir as people shifted in their seats.

"But you can fight the devil. You can close down Satan's party, you can shut the door in his face!" Uncle T.T. raised his hands straight up this time. "Stand up with me now and raise your hands to God. Stand up to the devil and tell him to *be gone!*"

I stood as I heard the people standing behind me. "That's right," Uncle T.T. said, and his voice filled the church. "Now say it with me. Satan, *be gone!* Satan, *be gone!*"

The voices rose all around me, and I found myself joining in. "Satan, be gone! Satan, *BE GONE!*"

"Thank you, brothers and sisters. If we stand together, we can send Satan a message. We may not save the world here tonight, but we can take that first step. We can show the devil that he is not welcome in our midst. I am here to make a crusade against him. But I am going to need your help. Dig down into your pockets, I beg of you, and make an offering that will help us spread the word."

Mom started playing "Onward, Christian Soldiers," as Matthew, Mark, and Luke came down with the offering baskets. Dad never used that hymn, so I was pretty sure Uncle T.T. had chosen it. Luke handed a basket to me. "That'll do it," he whispered. "Isn't he something!"

I nodded. T.T. Filkins was something, all right.

Chapter Eight

Dad says You were there in the church while Uncle T.T. was preaching. I felt Your presence, too — like energy all around us. Like electricity loose in the air. But it was Uncle T.T. talking, not You. Because Halloween wasn't a celebration of the devil, like he said, not when it was All Hallows' Eve, not even when it was Samhain. It wasn't a celebration of sorcery; it was protection against it. If Uncle T.T.'s wrong about that, he could be wrong about Halloween helping the devil, couldn't he? Couldn't he? I mean, maybe the world's as big a mess as he said, but it isn't because of Halloween!

After the prayer service I had nightmares all night. There were witches chasing me and devils throwing people on fires. When my alarm rang Thursday morning, I was trying to get away from a lion with horns. I had to lie there awhile, just looking at our old, comfortable, blue-wall-papered living room, to convince myself that it was all just a dream.

Uncle T.T. couldn't be right about Halloween inviting the devil into the world! I thought about all the little kids getting excited about their costumes and picking out just the right pumpkin to make into a jack-o'-lantern. And people decorating their houses and buying candy to give kids and staying home to answer the door. I thought about people taking pictures of babies in bunny suits and toddlers in witch hats. None of that was bad.

But those weren't the only things that happened on that night. What if Halloween *did* make the world a more terrible place? Even if the stories about poison candy or razor blades in apples weren't true, people really did set fires that night. There really was violence in some cities. Even though Halloween wasn't *meant* to celebrate the devil, did it help him anyway? Maybe I should go to school and tell them they couldn't use my script for the pageant. Brian would kill me. Mrs. Teator probably would too. I'd be letting everybody down and I'd be off the sixth-grade team forever. But wasn't that better than helping the devil?

I took my script out from under the couch cushion where I'd been keeping it and sat for a minute, just looking at it. It was just a play, and maybe a good one. I liked it. The other kids liked it. Everybody was pretty sure people would come see it and pay money that would go to UNICEF and help children all over the world. I'd done the research myself, and it didn't fit what Uncle T.T. said about how Halloween got started or what it meant. Even if it had started out as a pagan festival, Christians made it All Hallows' Eve so it would be a holy night when people thought about dying and prayed for the dead. That had to make it as much God's night as the devil's.

Finally I decided I couldn't decide. Not yet. What I needed was an answer—not one I thought up for myself, but a real one. A sign. Mom prayed for signs from God all the time, and she got them. Why couldn't I? So I got down on my knees and first I said the Lord's Prayer and then I asked God to send me a sign about which team I should be on—the sixth-grade team or the crusade team. In the meantime I'd do my best to work for both of them.

At breakfast everybody was bubbling over about how much money we'd taken in the night before. "More on one Wednesday night than we've taken in the last four Sundays combined!" Mom was positively glowing.

"That's only the first step," Uncle T.T. said. "We start small, but we build. I'll be on a radio talk show from Cleveland on Saturday night. And I'll speak again at the Sunday service. Meantime, we get the crusade posters printed." He turned on his from-the-pulpit voice. "'A little one shall become a thousand, and a small one a strong nation.'" He looked at Matthew, then at Mark. "Well?"

Matthew shrugged and shook his head. Mark too.

"Isaiah," Luke said.

"Right! Chapter sixty, verse twenty-two."

I could hardly believe my ears. Luke had known a Bible verse the twins had missed. When Matthew and Mark and I excused ourselves to get ready for school, Luke was still at the kitchen table listening to Uncle T.T. talk about what he'd say on the radio talk show. He hadn't even finished his cereal.

Besides praying, I asked for a sign every time I talked to Jesus. I wasn't sure what kind of a sign it would be, and I hoped I'd recognize it if it came. The signs in the Bible were easy. Nothing like that was happening, that was for sure. There were no burning bushes or wheels in the middle of the air. Thursday it rained all day, but there wasn't even a rainbow.

Things at school went on just the way they'd been going. We had blocking rehearsals Thursday and Friday after school and again Saturday morning, and by then we'd made it through all three acts. I could see how the whole thing just might work. It was beginning to look like a play.

There was a full-page ad for the crusade in the paper on Friday, and even though none of the kids mentioned it, I had a feeling some of them had seen it. I caught kids looking at me sometimes, the way they used to because of my clothes. Wondering, maybe. Friday afternoon David Prentice asked me if T.T. Filkins was related to me. We were on the playground and there was a lot of noise, so I pretended I hadn't heard him, and went to ask Nicole about some math homework. He didn't ask again.

At home everybody was so busy, they hardly noticed me. Whatever anybody asked me to do for the crusade, I did. All afternoon Saturday Mrs. Quigley and I baked for the fellowship hour after the Sunday service. We made three times as many goodies as usual, and even so, it turned out not to be enough.

The church was as full as I'd ever seen it, even on Easter. Uncle T.T. talked about the devil again, and it was just as scary and just as ferocious as before. Usually, lots of people go right home after the service. This time nearly everyone stayed for fellowship hour. After they shook hands with Dad, they all crowded around Uncle T.T., leaving Dad just standing there smiling. Finally he started clearing away used coffee cups and paper plates. By halfway through, Mom had to rush out to Kroger's for doughnuts. On her way back she stopped at St. John's Episcopal Church to borrow an extra coffee pot.

By Monday I'd managed to convince myself that things could work out just the way they had so far, that I could stay in the middle, a member of both teams, and nobody would notice. Or care. But the minute Mrs. Teator called the class to order Monday morning, Melissa knocked down that idea. She raised her hand and waved it so furiously that Mrs. Teator, who was still finishing checking the roll, had to call on her.

"My mother says that crazy man T.T. Filkins is going to wreck our pageant. Nobody'll come."

"T.T. Filkins. My mama and my aunt were talking about him—" Lashonda said, and turned around in her seat to look at me. "Is he any kin of yours?"

I gulped. There was no way to get around it this time. "He's my uncle. And he's not crazy."

Everybody started to talk at once, and Mrs. Teator stood up. "All right, class, let's have a little decorum. Has everyone heard about the Reverend Filkins's tent crusade?" Most of the kids had, but some hadn't. "Johnna, would you feel comfortable explaining it?"

Comfortable? *Help!* My hands were already cold and wet. I nodded, then swallowed a couple of times, trying to think of what to say. I started out by telling them about my father's church, and needing to have money to help people like the Gephardts. I told them that my uncle was a traveling evangelist and that his crusades made money for churches the same way our pageant was supposed to make money for UNICEF.

"So what's all this stuff about the devil, and Halloween making people violent?" Melissa asked.

"He believes Halloween is the devil's holiday," I said, and my voice squeaked. I swallowed again. "Because it's pagan."

"There isn't any such thing as the devil," David said. "My dad says that's just superstitious nonsense."

"Our priest says there's a devil," Nicole said.

"Yeah, but he doesn't have anything to do with trick-or-treating," Ethan said.

Brian held up his script. "But Halloween isn't pagan anymore. We show that in the pageant. *You* know that!"

I nodded. "I didn't say I believe it, I said he does." What I wanted to do right then was hide under my desk.

"So is Johnna's uncle really going to wreck our pageant, or what?" Jerome asked.

"The crusade may put Johnna in a difficult position," Mrs. Teator said, "but it could actually work for the pageant. The more people talk about Halloween, the more publicity they generate for us. After all, if Reverend Filkins's message is that Halloween is harmful because of its pagan origins, what better way to find out about those origins than to come to a pageant about its history? Bradyville has supported our Halloween projects every year. I see no reason why that should change now.

"We can stress the fact that every year the Sixth Grade

Halloween Project has benefited UNICEF. Surely no one can find harm in that. Lashonda, let's have a meeting of the publicity crew at lunchtime and discuss how we can take advantage of the situation. I'll gather the figures on how much we've donated to UNICEF in the last twenty-five years. We can put that figure on all our posters. Now, let's get on with language arts." Courtney Stubbins raised her hand. "Yes, Courtney, you had something to add?"

"I— my—" She stopped for a second, and then went on. "My mother says I have to drop out." She said it so fast it was hard to be sure of the words.

"You what?"

Courtney's neck was splotched with red and she twisted her fingers in her lap. "Drop out. She heard Reverend Filkins on the radio Saturday night, and she wanted to make me drop out right then. But I told her about UNICEF, and she decided I could stay. Then we went to the service on Sunday, and she changed her mind."

"I'm sorry to hear that, Courtney. You've been an excellent stage manager. You must be very disappointed."

Courtney nodded. She kept her head down, but I could see tears on her cheek. I thought about the blocking rehearsals, and Courtney's whistle. I thought about the way she'd gotten so she could tell people what to do. Even Kyle and Ethan and Jerome. And they listened. Courtney loved being stage manager, and she was good at it too. It was almost like she'd become a different person since we'd started rehearsals.

Mrs. Teator was talking about a replacement, but I wasn't listening. I was thinking about Uncle T.T.'s message. He said Halloween hurt people. But it hurt Courtney to have to drop out, didn't it? Really hurt her! And what she had been doing wasn't bad at all—it was good. For her and for the pageant. And then, all of a sudden, I thought that this might be the sign I'd been looking for. It wasn't a sign that proved Halloween helped the devil, it was one that proved just the opposite, that Uncle T.T.'s message was hurting a kid, a real kid, who hadn't done anything wrong.

"Surely there's someone willing to take on the stage manager's job."

I looked up. Mrs. Teator was peering at the class over her reading glasses. But nobody was saying anything.

"If no one wants to give up being on stage, how about someone who doesn't have an acting part?" Still there was no answer.

I looked over at Courtney. She seemed to have shrunk back down to the size she always used to be, back when it was hard to notice she was even a member of Mrs. Teator's sixth grade. I raised my hand. "I'll do it," I said. "I'll be stage manager."

Mrs. Teator took off her glasses and let them drop to

the end of their cord. "Are you sure, Johnna? Don't you think this could create some friction at home?"

Everybody was looking at me. The whole sixth-grade class, including Courtney. Including Brian. Yes, it could cause friction at home. But I'd been asking for a sign, and I felt sure I'd had it. *It* was *the sign I've been asking for, wasn't it?*

I nodded. "I'm sure. I'll be stage manager."

Chapter Nine

If Courtney having to quit the pageant wasn't the sign I asked for, I hope You'll find some way to let me know, and right away, because it's going to get harder and harder to change my mind. This sign business is very tricky. It would be lots easier if You could just talk to me and I could hear You.

Mrs. Quigley once told me she was so busy, she kept meeting herself coming and going. That's what I felt like the whole next week. At home there were fliers to get distributed and posters to put up all over town, envelopes to stuff and address, stamps to lick. The phone rang all the time with people asking what they could do. Mom was organizing what was starting to seem more like an army than a team of volunteers. It was Uncle T.T.'s crusade, but most of the time he wasn't around. He was off visiting other churches, doing radio talk shows, taping television programs. Whenever he could manage it, Luke went with Uncle T.T. He may have thought being a minister with a regular church was boring, but apparently Uncle T.T.'s life seemed anything but. Sometimes they didn't get home for dinner, which was probably fine with Luke, since whoever happened to be around usually had to fix it.

School was just as busy. Besides regular schoolwork, I had to learn all the stage manager's duties and figure out how to keep everybody in line the way Courtney had. I had to take notes for Mrs. Teator and give people their lines or remind them of their blocking if they forgot. I had to be sure everybody got to rehearsals on time and I had to keep track of what all the crews were doing. A lot of parents had gotten involved with the crews. Melissa's mother had five other mothers sewing costumes with her, and a couple of the fathers were helping build sets. Parents drove kids around to put up posters, and started selling tickets to their friends. So I had to keep track of what parents were doing too.

Sometimes I could hardly tell which team I was working for, there were so many things that sounded alike. Posters, lights, sound, borrowing stuff, renting stuff, getting volunteers, being sure they did what they'd promised to do. Still, I did my best to keep the crusade and the pageant far apart, and I absolutely never talked about one around anybody from the other.

"Things are sure heating up in this town," Brian said one day as we walked to school. "Mom says she's never seen so many letters to the editor in her life. People calling each other names, arguing about religion. She thinks we could end up with the whole town divided into warring camps. Like the Celts and the Romans." Brian was playing a Roman soldier in the first act, and he'd started carrying his wooden sword with him all the time. He used it now to whack a milkweed pod that exploded into feathery seeds. "One of the letters yesterday says the mayor should ban trick-or-treating."

"He can't do that, can he?" I asked.

Brian shrugged. "I don't know. It's not just Bradyville, either. Your uncle's getting talked about all over the place. Dad says he heard his name mentioned on a radio call-in show from Chicago. People were calling to say Halloween is the devil's holiday and it ought to be stopped. Then some other people called in to say your uncle's crusade ought to be stopped. Lots of name calling on that program too. Dad thinks it's funny, but Mom's upset. She says whenever religion gets into an argument it's apt to get nasty and violent. And our family should be extra sensitive about the whole subject."

"Why?"

"Because we're Jewish. We may not be super religious, but we're still Jewish and Jews know a lot about hatred and persecution. She says when people start talking this way, somebody always ends up getting persecuted. That's why nobody should be trying to stop anything. Your uncle has a right to his crusade and everybody else has a right to Halloween. And she wishes people would calm down."

"Me too," I said, and changed the subject.

After school the next Friday we finally got to have our first rehearsal in the high-school auditorium. When we went through the doors at the back, I caught my breath. It was beautiful—rows and rows of blue upholstered seats, and green carpeting. The stage was enormous, with dark-blue velvet curtains and a ceiling that looked miles high. As soon as we went in, Brian rushed up onto the stage. He looked up at the bars of lights overhead and twirled around in a circle. "This is terrific!" he shouted. "We can do *anything* here."

Ms. Cappelletti, the drama teacher, dressed in a black leotard and a bright print skirt, introduced us to the kids from the drama club who were going to help us. A boy named Hugh was in charge of lights, and he showed us what they could do. He turned on spotlights with different colors, and dimmed lights out and flashed them like lightning. When he turned them all the way out, it was so dark Katie screamed. Then everybody wanted to know how they'd find their way around the stage when the lights were out, and a girl named Vanessa showed us how they mark the floor with glow-in-the-dark tape so people can get where they need to be and put props in the right place.

Another boy, Jason, showed us a fire machine. It had a light and a drum of aluminum foil and strips of red and orange plastic that went around and around. When it was on, it really did look like a fire. Best of all was the smoke machine. Jason charged it up and put what he called "fog juice" in it. When he turned it on, it poured smoke—fog—everywhere. Brian walked around in it, waving his sword. It billowed and moved around him. "Samhain mist!" he said. "Graveyard mist! Fantastic!"

Vanessa showed me where the stage manager stood, way over on one side of the stage behind the blue curtains. There was a stand there, sort of like a pulpit, where I'd put the production book. It had a little shielded light so I'd be able to keep track of the script as the show went along, whether the stage lights were on or not. And I was to have headphones that connected with the light-and-sound booth up behind the audience. I'd whisper into the microphone on the headset to give the light-and-sound cues.

After we'd seen the way things worked, we had our rehearsal. Even without the lights and sound, even with kids still carrying their scripts while they said their lines, it was like a different play altogether. When we were done, Mrs. Teator, curls bouncing, congratulated everybody on our first on-stage rehearsal.

"We are the sixth grade!" somebody said, and we all joined in. After the third time, even Hugh and Jason and Vanessa were saying it with us.

When we left the high school, I picked up a stick, and Brian and I had a sword fight all the way to his house.

During dinner that night, Mom complained that we were all getting home too late from school. "I need everybody here just as soon as you can get home. I'm swamped." She looked straight at me, and I couldn't look her in the eye. "You're the one I could always count on, Johnna, and even you've been getting home later every day."

I concentrated very hard on making a straight line of mustard down my hot dog. "It's Mrs. Teator's project," I said. "Everybody's got to work on it. It's part of our grade." Luke's foot cracked into my ankle, and I pretended not to notice. It wasn't really a lie. The project did count for language arts.

"I'll quit the Young Pilots' Club," Luke said. "Models can wait. Just tell me what you need me to do."

"Dust," Mom said. "Vacuum. Fix dinner. Fold underwear."

Luke's face dropped about a mile. "Isn't there something I can do for the crusade?"

Uncle T.T. reached across the table and ruffled Luke's hair. "It's all for the crusade."

"We could quit the soccer team if you want," Matthew said. He wasn't about to be outdone by Luke. It took a minute before Mark nodded. Mark's a lot better at soccer than Matthew, and I figured he'd rather do just about anything in the world than quit the team. But what Matthew does, Mark does.

"I'd be pleased for any help y'all want to give," Uncle T.T. said, "but nobody should give up what's most special to them. There's more to life than this crusade. Remember the parable of the talents."

Mark sat up very straight. "If Matthew can quit soccer, I can."

"Neither of you is quitting soccer," Dad said. "You made a commitment to the soccer team for the full season, and I won't have you letting them down. This crusade is important, but so is your word. Just come home right after practice and be ready to do whatever is needed here." He smiled, and I realized I hadn't seen that smile for days. "Even folding underwear."

I took a long, deep breath. If Matthew and Mark were supposed to keep their commitment to the soccer team, it only made sense for me to keep mine to the pageant.

Later, when I was making the couch into a bed, Luke came into the living room. He had on the white dress shirt he'd taken to wearing all the time. Probably if he owned white pants and white shoes, he'd be wearing those, too. "Mom and Dad are so busy, they aren't paying much attention, but you're still right in the middle of that Halloween pageant. How come?"

I shoved the couch cushion farther over my script. "Because it's a class project."

"So? You helped write it. That's enough to get your grade. You ought to quit now."

"You worked on yours the whole time."

"Yeah, but Uncle T.T. wasn't in town then, doing a crusade against Halloween. How do you think it looks for a Filkins to be working on a Halloween pageant?" Luke picked up my pillow and fluffed it, as if he was doing me a favor, helping me make my bed.

I snatched it out of his hand. "That's all you care about, isn't it? How it looks? But what do you *believe*? When you worked on the Halloween fair, did you think Halloween was wrong?"

"Sure. Mom and Dad never let us go trick-or-treating."

"Right, but they did let you work on the fair—"

"I just took tickets."

"You worked on it. If they thought Halloween was as

bad as Uncle T.T. is saying, they wouldn't have let you do anything. Because *anything* for Halloween would be helping the devil. All Mom and Dad ever did was hold a church service for people who wanted to come on Halloween night. They didn't try to make other people stop celebrating it."

"Well, maybe they should have."

I just looked at him. "Do you believe every single thing Uncle T.T. is saying?"

He didn't even have to take time to think about it. "Why not? Look around, Johnna. There are lots of bad things in the world. It stands to reason the devil's got something to do with it."

"The devil, maybe, but not Halloween. Not jack-o'-lanterns and kids in ghost costumes."

Luke shrugged. "All I know is what Uncle T.T. says. The devil's in the world, and Halloween helps him. And if some reporter finds out that a member of our family is working on something called 'Ghosts, Goblins, and Ghouls,' they'll use it against Uncle T.T. and the crusade. You *have* to quit."

"Dad says we have to keep our word and stick with our commitments. I have a commitment."

"You don't have to stick with a commitment to something that's wrong. You know that, Johnna. And what about your commitment to your family? That ought to come first. You have to quit. If you don't, I'm going to talk to Dad about it."

Friction at home, Mrs. Teator had said. I hadn't expected it to be with Luke. I punched my pillow and dropped it onto the couch. "I'm not going to quit."

"Okay, then—"

"But you don't have to talk to Dad. I'll do that myself." My stomach twitched just thinking about it, but I didn't have much choice.

Luke frowned. "Promise?"

I nodded. "Just give me some time."

"How much?"

I wanted days, weeks—till after the pageant. "Till tomorrow night."

"Okay." He glanced at his watch. "But if you don't talk to him in twenty-four hours, I will." He started out and turned back in the doorway. "It's the right thing to do, Johnna."

I flopped down on the couch. How come everybody else thought it was so easy to know what was right?

Chapter Ten

I guess it was too much to hope I could be on both sides the whole time without any problem. I thought if I just worked on the crusade and didn't talk about the pageant at home, nobody would notice. What if Dad tells me I have to drop out? Honor thy father and thy mother. That means do whatever they say, doesn't it? So I guess I just have to find out what that is. If You were a regular, human best friend, I would ask You to go with me when I talk to Dad, to sort of be on my side. I hope You'll do that anyway.

Saturday morning we had another rehearsal at the high school. At breakfast I didn't tell anybody where I was going, just that I'd be back and ready to help by lunchtime. Luke gave me a look, but I ignored him. Dad was about to leave with Uncle T.T., so I couldn't talk to him yet anyway.

The rehearsal went pretty well. Some of the kids were learning their lines. I had to follow the script very carefully so I could prompt them if they forgot. I was surprised to find out that even though I'd written the lines myself, I couldn't remember them word for word. Mrs. Teator said by the time the show opened we'd have gone over it so often, I'd probably have it memorized, cues and all.

Brian had an orthodontist appointment after rehearsal, so I walked home alone. All the way, I thought about what I'd say to Dad. It was one thing to decide for myself that Uncle T.T. was wrong about Halloween, and another to tell Dad that. Especially since it meant I thought he was wrong too.

I could tell him about the sign, of course. But what if he said it wasn't real? What if he said I was misinterpreting—the way he says some people misinterpret the Bible? That was the trouble with signs. Even I couldn't be completely sure of mine, especially since it let me stick with the pageant, which is what I wanted to do anyway. It would have been easier to believe I'd understood a sign if it told me to do something I *didn't* want to do. I could use the commitment argument, but then he could say just what Luke said, that if you make a commitment to do something wrong, it's better to break it.

Help! The closer I got to home, the more scared I got. Dad would make me drop out. I just knew it. What would Mrs. Teator do if she lost another stage manager? Maybe Dad wouldn't be home yet. At least I might be able to put off telling him a little longer.

Dad's car was in the drive, but Uncle T.T.'s wasn't. That was okay—they'd been planning to go somewhere together. When I went in the back door, it was quiet. No telephones, no voices. Nobody home. I breathed a sigh of relief and opened the refrigerator door to see what there was to drink.

"Johnna? Is that you?"

I slammed the refrigerator door shut and jumped back as if I'd been caught doing something I shouldn't. Dad was in the dining room. I made my voice as calm as I could. "Yes, Dad, it's me."

"T.T.'s visiting a church in Canton on Sunday, so I'm preaching here. He dropped me off to work on my sermon." Dad came out, his sweatshirt sleeves pushed up, his hair mussed. "Not that anybody'll want to hear me after T.T., but I have to have something to say just in case somebody shows up."

"It's your church, Dad. Of course they'll show up. How's it going?"

He shook his head. "All I've got so far is my text—'Be kindly affectioned one to another with brotherly love.' Romans twelve, verse ten."

"What does that have to do with Halloween?"

Dad ran his hand through his hair and it ended up more mussed than ever. "Given the way people are talking to each other in this town, I thought this might be more useful. Besides, if I tried to talk about the same thing as T.T., I'd look pitiful in comparison."

"Dad!"

"Believe me, Johnna, it's true. I've had long experience with the phenomenon. I don't even mind anymore. Or not much." He grinned and waved toward the refrigerator. "Did you find anything good in there?"

I shook my head. "Just milk."

"So, pour yourself some milk and I'll have a cup of coffee. We'll take a little break."

When I had my glass and he had his cup, we sat down at the kitchen table. We sat in silence for a while, and I sipped my milk, trying to think what to say. Then I gave up and just started. "You know I've been working on the Halloween project for Mrs. Teator's class."

"So I understand."

"Well." I gulped the rest of my milk and set the glass on the table. I felt as if I were talking to Dad the minister instead of Dad the dad. "You remember her class does different projects every year—to raise money for UNICEF. Luke's year they did a fair, with a parade and a costume contest. And our class is doing a pageant—'Ghosts, Goblins, and Ghouls: The History of Halloween.'"

"I've seen the posters."

"Right. Well. I wrote it. And I'm the stage manager."

Dad didn't answer. He just sat there, one elbow on the table, his coffee cup in his hand, looking at me. He wasn't going to make this any easier.

"Luke says I should quit. Because of the crusade."

"I take it you don't agree with him."

I shook my head. "They really need a stage manager. If I quit, I don't know who would do it. Like you said about the twins and soccer—I made a commitment. And anyway, it's a regular class project. We get graded."

"Are you telling me that if you quit, Mrs. Teator would give you an F?"

Dad was too smart to be fooled by excuses like grades and commitments and UNICEF. "Uh—no. The thing is, I don't want to quit. I like Halloween, and I always have." I decided to tell him the whole thing, my kindergarten mommy costume, and my prize, and all the other costumes since. "I've always done Halloween at school," I finished. "I knew you wouldn't like it, but it didn't seem like such a bad thing. And it wasn't. It was fun. So was the pageant, till Uncle T.T. came and started the crusade."

"Have you been listening to what T.T. says?"

"Yes. But Brian Stern and I did a lot of research for the pageant. We show the whole history of what Halloween has been from the Celts through the Romans

101

and the Christians and clear up to now. And I don't think Uncle T.T.'s right." I stared at a ring of white on the table where my milk glass had been. "It isn't the devil's holiday. It never was."

Dad put down his cup. "Did you know that there are people who worship the devil? And did you know that Halloween is their most sacred night?"

I nodded. "But there aren't very many people like that. For most people Halloween isn't about God or the devil, either one. It's about parties and dressing up and trick-or-treating. Besides, stopping Halloween wouldn't keep people from worshipping the devil if that's what they want to do. It would just keep everybody else from having any fun."

"And you don't accept the idea that using all those symbols, of witches and devils and demons, encourages Satan, sets up an atmosphere in which he can thrive among us?"

I moved my glass until it was exactly in the middle of the milk ring. "No. I really don't believe that."

Dad took a sip of coffee. "What do you believe, Johnna?"

I picked at a hangnail on my thumb and thought for a minute. "I believe that Halloween isn't just not evil. It's good. Important. Kids like it more than any other holiday except Christmas, and maybe part of it is the fun of dressing up and part of it is getting candy. But we talked about it in class, and we think the scariness is important too. Kids—and maybe everybody else, too—like to get scared of stuff they know isn't real, because it helps them not be so scared of stuff that is."

There was a silence. A long, long silence. Dad's face didn't change. I wanted to look away, but I didn't. Finally he spoke. "You've thought about this pretty hard."

"And prayed about it too." I picked at the hangnail some more, and it started to bleed. Then I told him about Courtney having to quit because of Uncle T.T.'s preaching. I told him how much working on the pageant had meant to her and how good it had been, and how much it had hurt her to have to quit. And then I explained about the sign. "I believe it was the sign I'd been praying for. Maybe there *are* some bad things about Halloween. But there are bad things about Uncle T.T.'s crusade, too. And I believe I'm supposed to work on the pageant. I believe it's right. I do. Uncle T.T. will have his crusade, and we'll have the pageant, and people could go to both and decide for themselves." There. I sat back in my chair. I'd told him everything I could. Now it was up to him.

He picked up his coffee cup and held it in both hands for a minute, as if he wanted to warm his hands. "Johnna, have you ever wondered why we live in Ohio and T.T. lives in Texas?"

I couldn't figure out what that had to do with Halloween, with me and the pageant. I shook my head.

"You know the Filkins family has been a preaching family for four generations." He paused and stared out the window over the sink. "In any other generation this conversation would lead one place and only one place. My daddy or his daddy or his daddy before him would have answered you so fast it would have made your head spin. They'd have told you to quit the pageant. And they'd have taken a switch to you for getting into it in the first place. T.T. would tell you the same thing, though he'd probably skip the switching part. The Filkins family knew the Word, and they knew what it meant. There wasn't any other way to look at things." He put his cup down.

"The trouble was, I didn't always hear the Word exactly the way the others heard it. I still don't. It's a matter of which parts of the message come across louder, maybe. The differences aren't very big, Johnna. But even so, while our father was alive there wasn't room for them. Not there, in his home." He picked up my milk glass and his cup, shoved back his chair, and stood. "So your mother and I came here, to begin our own preaching family. T.T. stayed, of course. T.T. heard the Word just the way Daddy did, and besides that, he had the gift. He was the best of all of us at getting that Word to the people."

He took the dishes to the sink and then turned back

to me. "You know how I feel about Halloween. I don't want you to participate in any way. When you were little, you disobeyed simply in order to have a good time. If that's all you were doing now, I would say just what the others would say, that you had to quit.

"But you've thought about it hard. You've asked important questions. I can't tell you whether your sign was a real one, or where it came from. I do know that no matter what, someday you'll have to make your own choices. Just like I did. It seems a little early, but maybe you have to start now."

He came over to the table and stood behind me, his hands on my shoulders. "You know the verse 'If a house be divided against itself, that house cannot stand'?"

I nodded.

"I think it's only true if the divisions create a battle. I don't like battles—it was one of the Filkins family disagreements. I don't want a battle in my family. I hope we can manage to avoid that here." I nodded. "There's another verse too few people remember. 'Great men are not always wise.' Job thirty-two, verse nine." He squeezed my shoulders. "If even great men are not always wise, think how seldom the rest of us are.

"Luke's right about one thing, though. It's going to be awkward if the press gets the story that you wrote the pageant."

I thought about the front of the program Lashonda had designed. "Written by Johnna Filkins and Brian Stern," it was going to say. Just seeing the design had given me a little shiver of excitement. Inside the program, as stage manager I was to be listed right after Mrs. Teator as director. I said, "I could be sure my name doesn't show up anywhere, if that would help."

"Okay."

It wasn't until then that I realized how much I'd been looking forward to seeing my name in print. Vanity. For sure that was vanity.

"Things could be a little rocky at home, though. You'd best be ready for that." He went to the dining-room door and held it open. "You will still work on the crusade, won't you? We need you."

I wiped my damp hands on my skirt and nodded. "I've been doing both things so far."

Dad smiled. "I suppose my daddy would say it serves me right to have a dissenter of my own. It's time to get back to my sermon. I may not preach as well as T.T., but if I work at it, I'm a pretty decent writer."

I sat where I was until the door to the dining room swung shut.

Chapter Eleven

Mom says worrying is a waste of time, because what you worry about is hardly ever the thing that happens. That was sure true about telling Dad. Thanks. What I didn't worry about was everybody else in the family. Luke's mad that I didn't have to drop out, so he's making a big deal about not talking to me. Matthew and Mark and Mom and Uncle T.T. aren't so obvious, but I feel sort of shut out. It's like I'm somebody hired to help with the crusade, not really part of things. Not family. It feels awful.

Thursday, the day before the crusade began, Mrs. Teator gathered the whole class together at the front of the stage before rehearsal. She said it looked as if her prediction was coming true—our pageant was getting lots of publicity right along with the crusade. A letter to the editor that very morning had said people should come see our pageant before making up their minds that Halloween was a bad thing. And she'd heard the pageant mentioned on a couple of the talk shows, too. "I've even had a request from a TV station in Cleveland to let them videotape part of our performance"—she waited till the cheers died down—"to represent the other side in a documentary about the crusade."

Everybody cheered again. Even though Brian had already talked about having the pageant videotaped, he got so excited about the thought of some of it getting on a real television show, he fell right off the edge of the stage.

"There's another side to this though," Mrs. Teator added when everybody had settled back down. She held a couple of envelopes in the air. "We've received some rather—venomous—letters accusing us, me in particular, of doing the devil's work. I won't share them with you, because they're quite unpleasant. I understand that our principal, Mr. Lehman, has received quite a few such letters, and the superintendent's office has had even more. The atmosphere in this town, and well beyond this town, has become a little more heated than any of us could have expected."

"I'll say," Lashonda said. "I found some of our posters painted over with spray paint this morning."

"That could have been last year's class," Ethan said.

"They're jealous." Some of the boys started arguing about that.

Mrs. Teator held up a hand for quiet. "Kirby Maxwell came to me this afternoon and explained that he, too, was going to have to drop out. We won't have to cover his part, because he had no lines. But I want you to know that if any one of you feels that what we are doing challenges your religious beliefs, or makes life too uncomfortable for you in this community, you have an absolute right to quit, no matter how important your role. I only ask that you do it now so that we have time to find a replacement."

Nobody said anything. My life was uncomfortable, all right, but not Kirby or Courtney or half the class quitting was going to make me change my mind. I had a feeling that everyone was looking at me, but I kept my eyes on the production book so nobody would think even for a minute that I was going to quit. I'd have to miss two rehearsals because of the crusade, but that was all.

"Okay. Let's get on with it then. Johnna?"

I gave a toot on the whistle. "Places for act three."

We were trying out all the lighting cues for this act, so I took the production book to the stage manager's lectern backstage and put on the headset. Vanessa was already there, to help in case I made a mistake. Hugh was up in the light booth, helping Eric Griffith the same way. "Keep one eye on the stage and one on the script," she said. "And remember to give the warning a beat or two ahead of the actual cue. Nothing to it."

By the time we got to the end of the act, I was feeling pretty good. The kids had remembered most of their lines, and I hadn't goofed a single cue. Even from where I was, clear off to the side, I could see how well the lights were going to work. "Samhain, the Celtic god of death, is long gone," Jerome said, standing in a green-tinted spotlight on the otherwise dark stage.

"Cue Samhain spot," I whispered. "Number fifty-seven, go." Slowly a pale-blueish light came up on Jamie at the top of the ladder. The ladder began to move down toward the empty audience seats, rumbling as it came. Jamie kept his arms out—he had a belt around his legs to keep him balanced on the top rung. I could see Danny and Chris pushing from underneath, but the gigantic black robe Mrs. Gallagher had made hid them and the ladder from the front. Jason had rigged a special microphone so that when Jamie said his line, it echoed spookily. "But death is still here!"

Jerome waited, as Mrs. Teator had told him to, until the last echoes died out. "And we are still afraid."

"This is where you'll cue the music when it's ready," Vanessa whispered.

I nodded. "Lights out," I said. "House lights to half, house up." It was over. I wiped sweat from my forehead.

Once the sound crew had finished making the music tape, I was going to have even more cues to keep track of.

"You did good," Vanessa said, patting my shoulder.

"It's all so complicated."

"And from the audience it has to look so easy. Theater magic! Isn't it great?"

I took off the headset and turned off the light on the lectern. She was right. It was great.

Brian chattered nonstop all the way home, mostly about the television station that wanted to film the pageant. He was practically ready to accept an Emmy for the script by the time we got to his house. I caught his excitement, even though my name couldn't be on it. From his house to mine, I was thinking about the possibility that something I'd written, with or without my name, might get on TV. The crusade was the farthest thing from my mind, so I was surprised when I turned the corner for home to see that the rented crusade tent was up.

It was white, and it covered most of the vacant lot. Trucks and vans were parked around it, and people were hurrying back and forth. The side flaps were rolled up and I could see people inside, setting up folding chairs, running wires, and carrying lights and sound equipment. It reminded me of the first technical rehearsal we'd had for the pageant.

Luke was on his way from the tent to the house. His

face looked just the way Brian's had on the way home, as if somebody had turned a light on inside. He saw me and started to say something, then must have remembered he wasn't talking to me, because he just brushed past. But I could tell he was so excited, it had almost been worth sharing it with Johnna the traitor. Later I found out what it was. Uncle T.T. had decided to let the boys preach with him at the crusade. Matthew was to be first, on Friday, then Mark on Saturday and Luke on Sunday. He'd given them each ten minutes and told them they could say anything they wanted.

Much as I hated talking in front of people, I felt a twinge when I found out the boys were getting to preach. I'd been left out again. Was it because of the pageant? Or was it, as usual, that I was a girl?

We all stayed home from school on Friday. It was a bright, crisp fall day, and right from breakfast at about dawn, the tension started building. Would the weather hold? Would there be enough people to fill the tent? The boys kept disappearing, and I figured they were all trying to work on what they were going to say when they got their ten minutes to preach.

I just hung around and did whatever anybody needed. Most of the afternoon I spent with four women I didn't even know who'd come from another church to help. We unpacked and ironed the white robes Uncle T.T. had rented for everybody who was going to have any part in the tent meeting—the choir, the ushers, even the security guards. Lots of those people too were coming from other churches. The robes were perfect. No stains, no worn spots. They weren't anything like the old navy-blue ones we use for regular church services.

We were all supposed to be at the tent an hour early, but the boys were so excited, they gobbled their dinner, dressed, and were gone half an hour before I even started getting ready. By the time the service started, they'd probably be so wrinkled, all the ironing would be a waste. I was combing my hair when Dad came to check the mirror. A red satin stole embroidered with white designs hung around his neck and down the front of his robe. "I'm not used to wearing one of these. Is it even?"

I gave one side a tug so that the tassled ends were the same distance above the bottom hem of the robe. "Now it is. You look terrific."

Dad shook his head. "I'll never get used to all this fuss about how things *look*."

"It's like a costume. T.T. says people want the image to be just right."

"I know. But the Word of God doesn't need an image."

"Mom says image is T.T.'s thing and he knows how to

use it. It doesn't change the Word, it just helps some people hear it."

Dad sighed. "Right. That *is* the point, after all—for people to hear the Word. I have to remember that."

We left the house a few minutes later. Our driveway was taken up by two light-blue school buses, from the True Bible Sunday School. Cars and pickup trucks, campers and buses, lined both sides of the street as far as I could see, and groups of people were heading for the tent on foot, some of them carrying Bibles, some of them carrying picnic baskets or coolers.

By the time we got near the tent, I felt as if we had joined a river of people. "A Mighty Fortress Is Our God," the hymn Mom was playing on a big synthesizer, boomed out from the loudspeakers set up inside the tent and hanging on the outside from each main support pole. Matthew appeared, struggling to carry four metal folding chairs under each arm. "At this rate, Uncle T.T. says we'll overflow." He rested the chairs on the ground. "Here, Johnna, take some of these. Another truckload just arrived and we've got to roll up the tent flaps and get all the chairs set up around the outside."

For the next half hour I didn't have time to think about much of anything except how to carry chairs without tripping on my robe, and how to work my way around the outside of the tent against the flow of people looking for the entrance. I had to keep an eye out for the electrical cables, which snaked everywhere over the trampled grass. By the time the service was scheduled to begin, every chair inside the tent was filled and the four rows outside the rolled-up flaps were filling quickly.

"Where did all these people come from?" I asked Matthew.

"All over the state. And Mark says he's counted license plates from five other states besides!"

Luke joined us. His collar was out of place and his hair was mussed. "I overheard somebody say he'd driven all the way from Waukegan, Illinois, just for this."

"There won't be anybody left for tomorrow night or Sunday," I said.

"Tell her of course there will," Luke said to Matthew, and stepped out of the way of a family who wanted the chairs he had just put down. "Uncle T.T. says lots of them will just come again. Some families make a whole weekend of it."

"I wonder if they give money every night," Mark said.

"He says they will if they like the show."

The show. That's what it was, just like the pageant. There was even a stage manager—a man who stood outside the tent wearing a headset and talking to Mom, who had an earphone in one ear as small as a hearing aid and a tiny microphone pinned to the collar of her robe. The head usher and the head of security had them too. The stage manager's job here was the same as mine at the pageant, to keep everything working smoothly, all the complicated stuff looking easy.

It was time to join the processional. I was part of it because I was helping to pass the collection baskets. The choir—made up of our own and two from other churches—was to go in first and arrange themselves on the risers set up on the stage. Matthew, Mark, Luke, and I were next. We'd sit on either side of the rented white pulpit. Dad was last.

The sound of crashing cymbals came from the synthesizer, and the noisy crowd began to get quiet. Drums and then cymbals again, and then, with the synthesizer set for the sound of a pipe organ, Mom started "Onward Christian Soldiers."

"Your collar," I whispered to Luke. He straightened it, and I checked my own. Everything seemed okay.

"Left," Matthew whispered. "Left, right." In step, we went through the tent flap into the blazing light inside.

I felt the crowd more than I saw them, as we went across the front of the stage. Finally we reached our chairs and turned to stand at attention in front of them. Then I could see the faces—an ocean of faces. The lights on us were so bright, I couldn't really make out individuals. If anybody I knew, anybody from my class, was out there, I couldn't tell.

The processional ended with a final cymbal crash. "Heavenly Father," Dad's voice boomed out. It seemed to come from everywhere in the tent at once, and from outside, too. I bowed my head and closed my eyes.

When the first hymn was over, Dad introduced Uncle T.T., "the Voice of the Living Word." Just like the first time, the crowd applauded and then got quiet and restless when he didn't appear.

"Go!" I heard the whisper of the stage manager into his microphone, and at almost the same moment Mom's hands moved on the keyboard. A trumpet blared.

"The harvest is past," Uncle T.T.'s voice came as the trumpet faded away. Without being loud, it seemed to reach right into your head, to vibrate your bones. "The summer is ended, and we are not saved."

Uncle T.T. came down the center aisle, a spotlight making his white suit almost shimmer. "Get thee behind me, Satan! Get thee behind me, Satan. Say it with me. Get thee—" The crowd joined in, and the tent seemed to shake with the sound. "One more time! Get thee behind me, Satan!"

No question—it was going to be a very good show.

Chapter Twelve

I don't have to tell You how successful the crusade was—You were there all three days. Dad's already got two new projects to use some of the money for. And it isn't only the money, either. People know about our church now who didn't before. Uncle T.T. says the real surprise was Luke. Matthew and Mark preached pretty well, but Luke was terrific. Not terrific for a kid—really terrific. It was a super weekend, I guess. Except that I can't get as excited as everybody else, even though Luke's talking to me again and things are almost back to normal. I have to say thanks for how it went, but it's a little scary, too.

At breakfast on Monday nobody could talk about anything except the crusade. Mom had gotten up early and written checks for every single bill we owed. She didn't even blink when Dad suggested putting a down payment on a house that the church could keep as a short-term shelter for whoever might need it. And everybody told Luke what a great job he'd done the night before. Even Matthew and Mark, who were probably jealous. Dad said Luke had the Filkins preaching gift. "One to a generation."

We thought Uncle T.T. was sleeping in, but he showed up halfway through the French toast, already dressed. "Doesn't anybody get the paper off the porch around here?" He tossed the newspaper into the center of the table. I had no problem reading the front page headline even upside down—GHOST-BUSTING PREACHER BLASTS HALLOWEEN. I couldn't cheer along with everybody else.

The crusade was just about the only topic of conversation at school, too. Only there, it was what I'd been afraid of—nobody was happy. "My father says your uncle ought to be run out of town," Melissa said the minute I walked into class. Before I could think what to say to that, I was surrounded.

"Yeah, but it's too late," Kyle said. "They should have run him out before that stupid crusade started."

Lashonda agreed. "Mama and Aunt Shawnie had a big fight about it yesterday. Mama said she was thinking of keeping us all home from trick-or-treating this year, and my aunt said if she did that, she'd come kidnap us and take us herself. You shoulda heard them yell. Aunt Shawnie won, though."

"Kelly Shaw says she heard the governor might ban trick-or-treating all over Ohio," Katie said.

Brian came in from the hall just then. "Don't be stupid. What does Kelly Shaw know? And who ever listens to fifth graders anyway?"

The final bell rang and Mrs. Teator came hurrying in, carrying a stack of pink slips of paper. "Take your seats, class." I was glad to be able to go back to my desk.

"Can the governor ban trick-or-treating?" Katie asked.

Mrs. Teator waited for everyone to sit down. "I think it's safe to say that's only a rumor." She held up the pink slips. "These, however, are real. They're telephone messages. The phone in the school office has been ringing steadily since six forty-five this morning."

"What do they say?" Jerome asked.

"They vary. In general, however, the message is pretty clear. It has to do with bringing the devil into the public schools. So before we begin our regular work this morning, I think we need to take a few minutes to discuss a topic we don't usually discuss in class. How many of you are Christians?"

"Do you only mean Christians like T.T. Filkins, or does that include Presbyterians?" Ethan asked.

"Presbyterians, Methodists, Baptists, Catholics—any Christian denomination."

I looked around as I raised my hand. Most of the other kids had their hands up, but not all.

"How many of you are Jewish?"

Sarah Goldman and Brian raised their hands.

"Moslem? Buddhist? Hindu?"

Only Jerome raised his hand. But after he put it down, David Prentice raised his. "What if you're not any religion?"

Mrs. Teator nodded. "That's an important point, David. Several of you haven't raised your hands yet. Americans are guaranteed the right not only to belong to whatever religion we choose, but also to belong to no religion at all. And each of us has a right to express our convictions or our doubts."

"Does that mean T.T. Filkins has a right to try to get Halloween banned?" Jerome asked Mrs. Teator, but Brian jumped up from his desk to answer.

"He has a right to try, but everyone else has a right to protect it. One person's rights end where the next person's begins. My dad says that's the whole point of the Constitution and the Bill of Rights—to keep people from being stomped on. By the government or by each other."

Before Mrs. Teator could say anything, the intercom crackled, and Mr. Lehman's voice, sounding very serious, interrupted. "May I have your attention please?"

Sometimes, just to be funny, Mrs. Teator says no, but this time she didn't. For some reason, I could feel my stomach clenching up. "I have just received a memorandum from Dr. Chandler, the Superintendent of Schools. All Halloween activities in the Bradyville public school system have been canceled. I repeat, all Halloween activities have been canceled."

Nobody in our class made a sound. We just sat there, staring at the intercom. Even through the closed door, though, we could hear the groans and shouts that went up from the other classrooms.

"He can't do that!" Jerome said. "Can he?"

Mrs. Teator sat down at her desk. She pushed the pink slips to the side, then picked them up and dropped them into the waste basket. "I'm afraid he can. I'm afraid he has."

"So what about the pageant?" Lashonda asked.

Mrs. Teator put on her reading glasses. For a minute she looked at the class notes that were spread out in front of her. Then she took her glasses off again. She shook her head. "It's a Halloween activity, class. So I gather that means it's canceled."

After lunch, which I ate in a corner with Brian, he asked everybody in our class to meet outside on the playground. He said it was pageant business, and urgent. Nobody but Brian was talking to me, as if the whole thing had been my fault, but I went anyway. I had as much riding on the pageant as anybody. More. Even though it was gray and cold and windy, nearly everybody showed up. We all stood in a shivery huddle around Brian.

"Mrs. Teator says there's nothing we can do, because the theater at the high school is public-school property. But Jamie and I had an idea. Dr. Chandler only has control over the schools. He can't stop us if we have our pageant someplace else."

"Where could we have it? There isn't anyplace else," Kyle said.

Jamie stepped into the middle of the huddle with Brian. "My uncle's the director of the community center. There's a stage at one end of the big gym. And curtains. And some lights. I called him from the office a few minutes ago and he said we could use it. Technically we have to rent it, but he'll only charge us ten dollars."

"It won't be quite as good as it would have been at the high school," Brian said, "but we can still do it. And I bet a whole lot of people would come. We'd get even more publicity if we went ahead with it now."

"Will Mrs. Teator still be the director if we do it there?" Nicole asked.

"She needs some time to see if she can get Dr.

Chandler to change his mind—about the pageant, at least. For now she suggested Johnna and I could take her place."

I expected everybody to object to me even helping to direct, but nobody said anything. A gust of wind caught some dust and swirled it up around us.

"Well?" Brian asked.

"Can you guys do it?" Lashonda asked.

"Johnna's doing okay as stage manager," Brian said. "And everybody already knows how it's supposed to go. I think we can."

I nodded. I did know what all the actors and the crew were supposed to do, at least. And nobody else seemed to want to try. "We'll do our best."

I wasn't sure they were quite ready to forgive me for the crusade, but for now it seemed to be the pageant that mattered.

"What about all the technical stuff? We don't know how to set the lights and work sound over there—"

"I'll call Vanessa," I said. "I bet the Drama Club will still want to help us. They'd probably rig lights in some-body's garage if they had to."

"Yeah. The high-school kids'll be P.O.ed," Jerome said. "Their Halloween costume ball must have been can-celed too."

"We can have our first rehearsal at the center tomor-row," Brian said.

"All right!" Jerome said, and the other kids cheered.

On the way home from school that afternoon, Brian wasn't his usual bubbly, bouncy self. He just walked along, scuffing his feet on the sidewalk. Finally I asked him what was the matter.

"It isn't enough." He stamped a foot and stopped walking. "It just isn't enough to get around the ban and do the pageant anyway. Because it isn't only the sixth grade. What about kindergarten kids with their first costume parade? What about all the other class parties and the decorations and the prizes? The schools belong to everybody, not just to a few people who don't believe in Halloween. It's not fair."

I thought about the red-crayon costume I'd wanted in kindergarten, the award I still had—now hidden under Uncle T.T.'s clothes in my dresser drawer. "You're right. It's not."

"Now listen. Your family wants to stop Halloween because they say it's the devil's holiday. Isn't that right?"

"Yeah."

"And that's probably why the superintendent has banned it—because of all those people saying we have to keep the devil out of the public schools."

"Yeah."

"Okay. That's a religious reason, isn't it? So stopping Halloween, which we know isn't a religious holiday anymore, for a religious reason, is mixing church and state.

Taking away Halloween because of your uncle's crusade—I'm sorry, Johnna—but that's unconstitutional and un-American. Like Mrs. Teator said, your uncle has a right to his religion, but he doesn't have a right to force it on everybody else."

"He didn't. It was Dr. Chandler who canceled Halloween."

"Yeah, but that's exactly what your uncle wanted."

I started walking again. Uncle T.T. *had* said the crusade was not just to warn people about Halloween, but to stop it. This wasn't just Courtney anymore. Or Kirby Maxwell. Their parents forced them to drop out, but that was because they believed Uncle T.T. Canceling Halloween in school took something away from everybody no matter what they believed.

Brian caught up to me. "I've got an idea. Mom and Dad say you can fight city hall if you know how. We can fight the superintendent, too."

"How?"

"We can circulate a petition among the kids. Saying we want Halloween back. Everybody'll sign it."

"What good would that do? Dr. Chandler isn't going to listen to kids."

"Maybe not, but their parents will. And Dr. Chandler'll listen to parents. I bet he only banned Halloween in the first place because he thought everybody wanted him to. All those letters and phone calls he got. I bet nobody called or wrote to *keep* Halloween, because nobody would even think we could lose it. We've got to show him how many people are on the other side. First we get the kids to sign, then we get them to take the petitions home to their parents and get adults to sign. We could get kids to take petitions door-to-door."

"How do you know we'd get enough signatures? Maybe most people really *do* want Halloween banned. Most of the letters to the editor were against Halloween. And it looked like most of Bradyville was at the crusade."

Brian shook his head. "Dad says it's a vocal minority. And the people who came to your uncle's crusade weren't just Bradyville people. They were what Dad calls true believers. They came for miles and miles. He took me for a walk to check out the cars. They were parked clear into our neighborhood, you know. And he was right. There were lots of Bradyville cars. But we counted license plates from twenty different counties. Also Indiana and Illinois and Kentucky and West Virginia. The way to find out what Bradyville people really think is to start a petition drive."

I thought about Dad calling America the greatest country on Earth. He says the Constitution is the greatest document ever written except for the Bible. If Uncle T.T. had a right to have his crusade and to say what he believed, and try to get something stopped, didn't everybody else have a right to use a petition drive to get it back? Dad would have to admit that was the American way. I agreed.

"Okay, then," Brian said, "it's settled. We organize a petition drive."

"We?"

"Of course. You and me and the rest of the class."

"I don't know—"

"It's perfectly fair. If we don't get enough signatures, we can't win. But we will get them. People want to save Halloween. But somebody's got to do the work. It's democracy, Johnna. Dr. Chandler made a decree like a king. Like a dictator. Why not let the people decide?"

I sighed. The American way. "Okay."

Chapter Thirteen

Brian's like a crazy person. He says nothing will make him give up. It's as if the whole ban on Halloween was aimed directly at him. Maybe it's because his family makes such a big deal about individual rights. First he stood up for Uncle T.T.'s right to say what he wanted. Now he says that no matter what, the superintendent has to give Halloween back. He reminds me of how ferocious You were about the money-changers at the temple. Righteous wrath, Dad calls it.

It wasn't as easy to start a petition drive as Brian thought it would be. First we had to write the petition. Or rather I had to—Brian still wouldn't write. I didn't blame him on this one. It wasn't easy. A petition has to explain the principle you want to stand up for, but it has to be short, so the people you're trying to get to sign will actually read it.

We had to decide whether we wanted to say Dr. Chandler was violating the Constitution, or whether we just wanted to say that we wanted Halloween back.

Brian's dad said we should look up the First Amendment if we wanted to bring freedom of religion into it, but when we did, we couldn't figure out how to write it in. Finally we just said, "We, the undersigned, demand that the traditional Halloween celebration be reinstated in the Bradyville public schools." It was as short and simple as I could make it.

The kids in our class signed right away, even Courtney, who said she didn't care if her mother found out. "She said I couldn't be in the pageant. She didn't say a thing about signing petitions."

But the other classes were harder. We had to try to catch them on the playground, and they didn't want to stop what they were doing to listen to us. The little kids didn't understand what petitions were all about, and when we tried to explain, they got bored and went back to the swings or their jump ropes. Brian started telling them if they didn't put their names on the piece of paper, they wouldn't be allowed to go trick-or-treating ever again. He got some names that way, but since it wasn't really true, I didn't think it was a fair way to do it. "We could pay 'em," Jerome suggested.

Kyle held up a fist. "How about I just tell 'em they have to?"

We decided to concentrate on older kids. But most of them didn't want to be bothered. They figured they could still wear their costumes to go trick-or-treating. We got signatures, but nobody wanted to take petitions home, let alone go door to door.

"My father says democracy spoils people," Brian said when a bunch of third graders had wandered off without even signing. "They figure somebody else'll stand up for their rights, so they don't have to do anything."

Finally a girl in the fourth grade said she would start a club called the "Save Halloween Club." I wasn't sure whether she really wanted to try to save Halloween or if she just wanted to have a club. At least all the girls took petitions home with them.

Even the sixth graders didn't want to get involved in the door-to-door stuff. "No time," Lashonda said. "I can hardly get all my pageant stuff done. We're gonna have to change all the posters to say it'll be at the community center."

"Organization," Brian said. "That's what we're going to need. And motivation. The kids need to be convinced there's a reason to make an effort. Mom and Dad are absolutely sure most people in this town want to keep Halloween. We just have to get petitions to them and give them a chance to say so."

Meantime, there was the pageant. All of the props and sets were still at the high school, of course. The drama-club kids were going to borrow a truck to bring everything to the community center, but they couldn't do that until the weekend. So we had to go back to the way we worked in the cafeteria, with masking tape on the floor.

The stage was pretty awful. There were curtains in the front, but they were old and dingy and torn. And there weren't any in the back, so instead of being able to put our set pieces up in front of plain black curtains, we were stuck with a concrete block wall painted a sort of mustardy yellow. When we tried to pull the curtains, they got halfway across and stuck. And when we turned out all the lights, nothing much happened because the room was all full of windows.

"We'll be doing it at night," Eric Griffith reminded everybody. "It'll be dark enough."

But he was pretty unhappy about the lighting system. There were only two light bars and a handful of stage lights. Jamie's uncle found us some masking tape and Lashonda helped me put it down, but we weren't sure we had everything in the right place. The stage was narrower and didn't go as far back, and everything looked so different it was hard to work out distances. We stuck folding chairs around on the stage where set pieces like the bonfires were supposed to go. "Just imagine the gravestones," I said.

"And the mist," Brian said. "Unless we figure out a way to do mist without the smoke machine, the whole audience is going to have to imagine the mist."

Getting ready to rehearse turned out to be the easy part. Once we got started, everything really fell apart. Nobody could figure out where they were supposed to be. The gym was so big that if people said their lines loud enough to be heard, echoes came back from the far corners. Kids who'd known their lines and all their blocking suddenly forgot everything.

Even if Brian and I had known how to direct, I wouldn't have been able to do it because I had to keep track of the script and tell everybody where they ought to be or give them their lines. And Brian just stood and watched, like watching a car accident you couldn't do anything about. Jamie didn't have his ladder, so he had to just walk downstage with his arms out, and there was no special microphone to make him sound like the god of death. When he said his first line, everybody laughed.

Finally even Jerome, who had been the first one to get all his lines learned and always, *always* did his part perfectly, forgot what act he was in and started his long second-act speech in the middle of act one. I started to tell him, and he just swore and jumped down off the stage.

"This'll never work!" he said, and kicked over a folding chair that made so much noise, the kids who were still trying to finish the scene just about jumped out of their skins.

"It'll be better when we get all the stuff here," Brian said. But half the cast was already following Jerome toward the gym door.

"Jerome Teazel, don't you dare walk outta here!" Lashonda shouted.

Everybody stopped and Jerome turned around. "You telling me what to do, girl?"

"Darn right I am!" She jumped down off the stage and ran up to stand practically nose to nose with him. "Want to make something of it?"

Jerome put his fists up. "You think you can stop me if I want to walk?"

Lashonda put her fists up, too. "I sure can."

Kyle took Jerome's arm. "Come on, you don't want to beat up a girl."

Jerome shoved him away. "No girl tells me what to do!"

I picked up my stage manager's whistle and blew it as loud as I could. In the big, empty, wood-floored room it just about broke everybody's eardrums. I went over and got between Jerome and Lashonda. There wasn't time to think. I just opened my mouth and started talking. "You're the druid," I said to Jerome. "And you're the very best actor we've got. Are you going to walk out and let Dr. Chandler beat us? Are you going to let him and Mr. Lehman tell us we have to be the first sixth grade in twenty-five years to miss our Great Teator Halloween Project? Are you?"

Jerome put his fists down. "What if it doesn't get any better? Look at this place. We'll never get it like the theater at the high school." A lot of the others agreed. "And I'm not making a fool of myself in front of the whole town. If we can't do it right, I don't want to do it at all."

"Right!" "Me either!" "No way!"

I blew my whistle again, not so loud this time. It shut them up. "You all listen to me. We are going to do it right. If we have to do it here, we have to do it here. But we'll find a way to make it so good, nobody'll even remember how it was at the high school. And anyway, the audience won't have seen it there. All they'll have is what we give them. If we give them a good show—a great show—they'll love it."

I went over and picked up the production book. "You see this? We've worked and worked and worked for this. It's our project. All of ours. Just ours. Not Dr. Chandler's, not Mr. Lehman's, not even Mrs. Teator's right now. This is *ours!*" I dropped my voice very low. "Do you really want to give up on it? Do you really want to sit back and let them take it away from us?" A couple of the kids said no. Lots of the rest shook their heads.

I let my voice get a little bit louder. "Every single one of you has worked to make this pageant a good one. And the kids from the drama club have helped us do it right. They're still planning to help, because they're mad at Dr. Chandler for trying to take our project away. They'll be here tomorrow. When they show up, you want them to see we've chickened out? When they come to work, you want them to see we've quit?"

More kids said no.

"Who are we?" I said, my voice low again.

"We are the sixth grade," Brian and Nicole and Kyle said.

"I can't hear you."

"We are the sixth grade." More kids joined in.

"One more time. Everybody. Who are we?"

"We are the sixth grade!"

The room echoed with the voices. They seemed to crash in on me. It was one of the best sounds I'd ever heard.

"Are we going to make this the best Halloween Project there ever was?"

"Yes!"

"Are we going to earn more money for UNICEF than any sixth grade class in twenty-five years?"

"Yes!"

"Are the grown-ups going to push us down and shove us around?"

"No!"

"Then come back here tomorrow ready to go to work!" I said. "Be on time and bring your props and anything else you think we need. The drama-club kids'll be here. We'll be here too." I put down the production book. The kids started to leave. "Who are we?" I yelled.

"We are the sixth grade!"

"It must run in the family," Brian said later, as we walked home. "That was preaching you just did."

Chapter Fourteen

Preaching, Brian called it, and I guess it was, sort of. What was amazing was how it happened. Like a miracle. It felt as if I just opened my mouth, and the words came. I didn't even have time to think what to say. I know this is strange, because I was talking about the pageant, about Halloween, that Uncle T.T. says is so bad. But for some reason, it felt as if the words were coming from You. Was it You? It was, wasn't it? This is what they mean when they talk about the gift. I have it too!

Brian kept raving about the way I'd "saved the pageant." He said I could get all the kids at school motivated to do the petition drive if I just talked to them that way. "You were terrific! Absolutely terrific! How come you never told me you could do that?"

"I never knew it. Anyway, I'm not sure I can," I said.

How could I explain that it wasn't really me? I couldn't very well say I thought it was Jesus talking. He'd think I was nuts. Maybe I was.

"Of course you can. You did it once, you can do it again. We are on a roll!"

Easy for him to say. What if the next time I tried, the words weren't there and all I could do was squeak? If a miracle happened once, did that mean it would happen again?

"Tomorrow," he said as he went up the walk to his house. "We'll go after the fifth grade tomorrow."

At home the vacant lot was full of people again, taking down the tent. The crusade had turned out to be nearly as much trouble to get over as to get ready for. Everything had had to be taken apart and packed up and taken back. There'd been tons of litter to pick up and we were going to have to reseed the grass where it had been trampled. But there were plenty of volunteers. Uncle T.T. was working on setting up a network of little churches like ours all over the state.

I wished I could ask him about the preaching gift. How it happened. What it felt like, and when he'd first known he had it. How he knew what to do with it. If it *was* a gift, then it was for doing good in the world. But what was good? If the gift came from God, and if I had it too, how could T.T.'s work against Halloween and mine work for it? I couldn't talk to Uncle T.T. about it after all.

He'd probably say if it was a gift from God, I had to use it the same way he did and say the same things.

Anyway, Uncle T.T. had gone to Cleveland to talk to a group of ministers that afternoon, so it was just us at the dinner table. And chicken for dinner instead of tuna casserole or macaroni and cheese. Whatever else it had done, the crusade had sure improved our menu.

"Can you believe Dr. Chandler canceled Halloween?" Matthew said. "I bet nobody thought the crusade would work that well. We've got the devil on the run."

Mark spoke around a mouthful of chicken. "Yeah! The guys at the high school are having a fit about the Halloween dance. You'd think it was the prom or something."

I stared at my plate and didn't say anything. I could just imagine what everybody would say when they found out we were still doing the pageant—*I* was still doing the pageant.

"Now that the crusade's over, when's Uncle T.T. going to take that rest he's supposed to be getting?" Matthew asked, reaching for his second piece of chicken.

"Your mother was right," Dad said. "T.T. can't sit still for one day, let alone six weeks. He's booked solid around here clear till Halloween. And right after that he's going back to Texas to start a whole new crusade." Was I imagining it, or did Dad sound as if he'd be glad when Uncle T.T. went back?

"What theme is he going to use after Halloween?" Matthew asked.

"He doesn't know yet."

"How about 'Don't take Christ out of Christmas,'" Luke said.

Mom shook her head as she passed a plate of tomatoes. "That's been done too often."

"Isn't Christmas a theme just in itself?" I asked. "It's got everything—the birth of Jesus, the angels, the spirit of giving, peace on Earth."

"Everybody uses all that stuff," Mark said. "One reason Uncle T.T.'s so good is because he's different. That's what turns people on."

"Besides," Luke said, "where's the devil in that? Remember what Uncle T.T. said about a crusade getting people to fight the devil. Peace on Earth doesn't do that. And anyway, there isn't peace on Earth. Never has been."

I pushed the last of my mashed potatoes into a little mound. "There sure isn't much peace in Bradyville right now. Wouldn't it be better to remind people to try for peace on Earth instead of getting them to look for a fight?"

Dad sighed. "You have to remember, the fight he's recruiting for is against the devil, not against other people."

I wasn't so sure about that.

"And unfortunately," Dad went on, "it's hard to

motivate people with talk about peace. Like it or not, people do need to be motivated. There's work—a lot of work—that needs to be done in this world. T.T.'s job is to get people stirred up and excited enough to really do something."

Luke said, "Yeah. Contribute money."

"But then that's what his crusades are about—money. Not God. Isn't that backwards?" I asked.

Dad frowned and stirred his coffee before he answered. "Crusades are fund-raising events—"

"Like rock concerts for the homeless," Luke said.

"Not quite like that," Dad said. "They're fund-raising events, but that isn't *all*. They're still religious services. You saw people's faces at the crusade. You felt the excitement. Jesus works in the world through T.T. It isn't just the money they give. At a crusade people can be changed for life!"

"And don't put down money. The church needs it," Mom said. "Without money, how could your father help people? T.T. does one sort of thing, he does another. But Jesus works through both of them."

"I want to do just what Uncle T.T. does someday," Luke said, and his eyes were shining. "I'll have suits like his, and a car like his—and I'll travel all over the country getting people to jump up and make their pledge to fight the devil. Just like Uncle T.T. I'm going to be a recruiter for God."

Matthew nodded. "You could probably do it too."

"Right," Mark said. "And when we have our churches, we'll invite you to come give crusades for us."

"Yeah, so we can go out and buy houses for shelters."

"And trailers for people whose houses burn down."

"I know it looks as if the crusade has caused a lot of friction—a bit more than we expected," Dad said. "But its main purpose is to do good, and it has definitely done good."

"And it'll go on doing good, as we use the funds it raised," Mom added.

I remembered what Brian had said about every good thing having something bad about it. The crusade was good. But it was bad, too. Couldn't they all see that?

The next day Brian brought a wooden box onto the playground and set it on one end for me to stand on. It reminded me of a pulpit. He said his dad called it a soap box, except this one had held peaches. Like a pulpit, though, it was to get me higher than the kids I'd be talking to. It looked pretty wobbly. "Can't we put it on its side?"

Brian tipped it over. That was better. I stepped up onto it, and it creaked a little, but it held me. "I feel sort of silly."

"It's great. I'll go tell Kyle to gather up the fifth graders."

"I don't know what to tell them."

"Just the same kind of thing you said yesterday. Except talk about *their* Halloween project. Tell them if they don't fight for their rights, they won't have them anymore." Motivation, I thought. Just like Uncle T.T. "You'll be okay. Once you get started, it'll come."

Brian was right. It did come. Kyle, Jerome, Ethan, Brian, and David, each carrying a sign that said SAVE HALLOWEEN, herded most of the fifth graders over in front of me and then stood around the edges of the crowd so they couldn't get away.

First I told them how the ban on Halloween was keeping this year's project from being done the way it ought to be done. Then I reminded them that next year was supposed to be their year. "But it won't be your year. Not even for the ones who get Mrs. Teator. Not if this ban holds up." It worked the same way as before. I didn't have to think of what to say ahead of time—I just opened my mouth and out the words came.

At first some of the kids fussed about being forced to listen. A couple of boys tried to leave, but Kyle and Jerome stood in their way, with their arms crossed. It didn't take long, though, till they were listening. I could tell by the expressions on their faces that I'd caught them.

"They say we have to learn about the American system, about democracy and freedom. But they don't want *us* to have democracy. They don't want *us* to have freedom. Because we're just kids. Is that fair?"

"No!" Brian shouted.

"No!" Jerome and Kyle said.

"What do *you* think?" I asked the fifth graders. I looked from one face to the other, as if I were talking to each one separately. "Is that fair?"

"No," a couple of girls in the front said. Some kids farther back muttered a little and shook their heads.

"We're not allowed to do our project at the high school. They wanted to stop it altogether, but we're not letting them stop it. We're doing it anyway. That's this year, though. And that's us. *You'll* be sixth graders next year. If this ban sticks, none of you will even get to start a project!" I paused to let that thought sink in. "We're gonna fight the ban. Are you going to join us?"

There was no answer. Kids shuffled from foot to foot and looked at each other.

"Mrs. Teator's sixth grades have been doing projects for twenty-five years. Twenty-five years! Next year would have been the twenty-sixth. Do you want to be the first sixth grade in all that time that won't get to even *start* a Great Teator Halloween Project?" I kept my voice steady and firm, but not too loud.

"No," some of the fifth graders said.

I let myself get a little louder. "Do you want to be the first sixth graders in twenty-six years who won't have a chance to make a contribution to UNICEF to help children in the rest of the world?"

"No!" a few more said.

I raised my voice a little more. "Do you want everybody to say that *we* were the last sixth graders who had the nerve to stand up for ourselves? That your class is a class that can be pushed around and won't fight back?"

"No!" Now it seemed to be all the fifth graders shouting the answer. Other kids had joined the group. There were fourth graders, third graders, even a few little kids who must have been in first.

"Today they can take away Halloween in school. Tomorrow, they can take it away everywhere else. If we don't stand up to them, what's to stop them from banning trick-or-treating in Bradyville? Are we going to let them do that?"

"No!"

"Join us!" I said. "Help us. If we don't all"—I lowered my voice almost to a whisper—"all"—I paused, and they seemed to lean toward me to hear better. It was a trick Uncle T.T. used a lot. "Us and you and everybody," I said to the girl closest to me. I could feel the rest straining to hear.

I straightened up suddenly, and shouted, *"All of us!"* One of the littler kids jumped about a foot in the air. "If every single class in this school doesn't get together and fight for Halloween, we're going to lose it forever." I heard my voice getting louder, almost by itself. *"Do you want to lose Halloween?"*

146

"No, no, no!" the kids yelled back. Some started stamping their feet, and the others joined in.

"Save Halloween!" Brian shouted. "Save Halloween!" In no time everybody had joined the chant.

As the shouting continued, two lower-grade teachers came hurrying over and broke up the crowd. The kids went, but the chant didn't stop completely. It popped up here and there among little groups. "That was great!" Brian said, picking up the peach crate. "I told you you could do it!"

I couldn't stop grinning. I understood what Luke meant—it really was exciting to be able to get people turned on like that. And the sense that it wasn't just coming from me, that it really was a gift, just like Uncle T.T.'s, just like Luke's, made me feel better than I'd felt since Uncle T.T. first talked about his crusade. What I was doing, even if the rest of my family didn't exactly agree, was the right thing to do. I just knew it. It was bigger than me, but it was bigger than them, too.

Chapter Fifteen

Johnna Josephine Filkins. That's me. I looked in the mirror this morning while I was combing my hair, and even though what I saw was just the same, what I felt was different. Not a whole lot different, but enough. Like waking up one morning and finding you're an inch taller. Whatever happened, it has to do with You. And I'm going to need You to help me figure out what happens next.

Over the next few days the petition drive took off, not just at school, but all over Bradyville. Kids took petitions door-to-door and their parents started helping them. High-school kids, who wanted the Halloween costume ball back, helped too.

Brian's mother and father organized a group of PTA members, starting with a meeting at their house. They stressed politics instead of religion. They said that with school funding dependent on voters, Dr. Chandler had only banned Halloween because the crusade made him think the majority in Bradyville wanted it that way. The point was to prove otherwise.

There were still plenty of letters to the editor about Halloween, but now the numbers began to change. More and more were for Halloween. Some called Uncle T.T. an "extremist" and a "fanatic" and said people like him shouldn't dictate school policy; others just said more people wanted kids to have Halloween than didn't, so it ought to go ahead.

Meantime, our class was working on the pageant as hard as we could. Jamie's uncle had found some curtains that weren't quite so old, and he let us paint the back wall of the stage black. That was some help. Vanessa and Jason and Hugh and a whole bunch of the other drama-club kids came to every rehearsal and did what they could with the lights and sound. But it wasn't going to be as good as it would have been in the theater.

By Saturday morning Mrs. Teator had given up trying to get Dr. Chandler to change his mind about the pageant. "He wouldn't budge," she said when she showed up at the community center for our rehearsal. "He said a public school employee should not be involved with this project, and I told him he might be able to dictate what I could do in my classroom, but not what I could do with my free time. So here I am!" Everybody cheered, but Brian and I cheered loudest. Nobody knew better than we did how much we needed her.

On Tuesday there was a front-page article in the paper about the petition drive. There was a picture of Brian and four fifth graders holding stacks of petitions in front of the mayor's office, and the headline said CHILDREN'S CRUSADE TO SAVE HALLOWEEN. The photographer had wanted to get me in the picture too, but I said no.

Everybody at home knew I was still working on the pageant, and they were sort of grumpy about it. They didn't talk about it directly, but the boys made little jabs and cracks every so often. And Mom fussed about how late I was getting home all the time. Even Dad made it clear he wasn't happy. But he'd said I could make my own choice, so he couldn't very well make me stop. If they all knew how much I had to do with the petition drive, things would have been much worse, I was sure.

Luckily Uncle T.T. was mostly away preaching, and everybody else was so busy planning how to use the money from the crusade that they weren't thinking that much about Halloween anymore.

Then on Wednesday morning, October twenty-third, during language arts, Mr. Lehman's voice came over the intercom again. "May I have your attention please."

"No," Kyle answered, and Mrs. Teator shushed him.

"I am pleased to announce that we just received a call

from Dr. Chandler's office. The ban on Halloween activities in the Bradyville schools has been lifted." A cheer went up all over school. "The sixth grade may resume their rehearsals at the high-school auditorium and all costume parades and Halloween parties will go on as previously scheduled. Any student who for moral or religious reasons is reluctant to participate in Halloween activities may be excused for that portion of the school day."

The intercom crackled and went off. But almost instantly it went on again. "To Mrs. Teator's class," Mr. Lehman said, "I would like to extend my congratulations on a job well done. You have acted like mature and responsible citizens of your school and your community. More than a thousand signatures were gathered in the petition drive you began. In a community the size of Bradyville, that is some showing! And to every other student who worked to protect individual rights, congratulations to you, too."

The class went wild. I grinned but didn't join in. I sat very still at my desk, my eyes closed. We had won! We had actually won! *Thank You*, I started to say. Then I stopped. Did that mean Uncle T.T. had lost?

No. Because for the first time ever, they'd said that it was okay for people not to take part in Halloween activities for moral or religious reasons. It was a real choice, now—for everybody.

Mrs. Teator was calling my name. I opened my eyes.

Brian was standing in front of the class and everyone was looking at me. "Yes?"

"I just wanted to have the two of you up here for a moment." Mrs. Teator tugged at her suit jacket and bounced a little as I went to stand next to Brian. "Class, it would seem that though everyone did his or her part to keep our project going and to bring Halloween back to the other students of the Bradyville schools, it is Brian Stern and Johnna Filkins we have most to thank. No matter what pressures they faced, these two refused to give in and give up." Mrs. Teator began clapping, and the rest of the class joined in.

When the clapping stopped, Mrs. Teator asked if either of us had anything we wanted to say. I nodded. "Go ahead, then."

I looked out at the class—my class. I didn't have to worry right now about what they were thinking about me. In a strange way, that had been partly Uncle T.T.'s doing. "Sometimes since all this started, I wanted to apologize for my uncle because he was trying to tell everybody else what they should believe and how they should act." I stopped. The kids were sitting very still. Even Ethan and Kyle. "I know, because lots of you said that your religions are different from ours, and you don't agree with what my uncle said. The thing is, I think he had a right to talk about his beliefs, and even to try to get other people to believe them. But everybody else had a right to talk too. That's how our country's supposed to work.

"Uncle T.T.'s talk got Halloween banned, and our talk—and the petitions—got it back. I think that's the way it's supposed to work. And the best thing is we can go back to the theater. Now I *know* ours is going to be the best Halloween Project in twenty-five years!"

"We are the sixth grade!" Brian said. And everybody joined in.

Mrs. Teator let us go for a few minutes, and then she blinked the lights. "And now, class, we have only one week to get the pageant ready, so we'll have to—"

Lashonda suddenly let out a yell. "Oh, no! We gotta change all the posters all over again!"

I couldn't get the questions out of my mind, though. If Uncle T.T.'s preaching was a gift from God, and his message against Halloween came from Jesus, like he said, what about my gift?

Dad had told me I was old enough to make choices. And I'd made them. But as good as I felt about the petition drive and the pageant and myself, I still felt bad that I had had to take a stand that went directly against the whole rest of my family. I talked to Jesus about it, of course, but what I needed was a person to talk to. One who could answer.

Thursday night, after I'd fixed up my bed, I went into the dining room where Dad was starting to work on his next sermon. "Do you have a few minutes?"

"Sure." He waved a hand at the books jumbled around him on the table. "I don't even have a subject yet, so you're not interrupting any great thoughts. Sit." I pulled out a chair and sat. "What's up?"

"Uncle T.T. says there's two sides, good and evil, and he gives people a choice. Mostly they want to choose good."

"Right."

I rubbed at a spot on the table. It looked like a place Luke had spilled model glue. "I guess most people do want to choose good. But what if it isn't that easy? What if two different things both seem good. And also bad. What if every single choice has some of both—some good and some evil?"

"What sorts of choices?"

"You said the crusade did good. And I know it did. But it did something bad, too—it got Halloween banned in school. Not just for the people who don't believe in it. They banned it for everybody. So no matter how good the crusade might have been for us, it was bad for a lot of other people."

Dad made a tent of his fingers and didn't say anything.

"Uncle T.T. says he gets his message from Jesus. Not everybody believes in Jesus. Brian's Jewish. Jerome's Moslem. Some kids don't have any religion at all. And even most of the Christians in our class don't agree with you and Uncle T.T. about Halloween. So for them it isn't fair that the crusade got it banned.

"You always say this is the best country in the world." Dad nodded. "But in this country everybody's supposed to be able to believe what they want to believe, or not believe at all. On the sign in front of our church it says 'In Jesus Everybody is Somebody.' Do you believe that?"

"I do."

"Then it has to mean everybody, doesn't it? Jesus cares about everybody. *Really* everybody, not just people who believe what we do."

"Well, He *cares*. But that doesn't mean—"

I could tell by the look in his eyes that Dad was getting ready to start a sermon about that. Jesus saying "I am the Way and the Truth and the Life" or something. "Wait. Let me tell you what's been happening to me. And what I did."

First I explained about the community center and the terrible rehearsal and what happened that day when I started to talk. Then I told him about the petition drive. How working on the petition drive seemed to be a good choice. And about how I found out I could motivate people to do things by talking to them, just like Uncle T.T. Just like Luke.

"Are you suggesting I was wrong about the Filkins gift going to only one person in a generation?"

I nodded. "I think so. Uncle T.T. says he gets his message from Jesus. But that's how it felt for me, too. The trouble is, about Halloween we're on opposite sides. If Uncle T.T.'s right that there are only two sides, good and evil, then taking the opposite side the way I did with the petition drive would be evil. And it wasn't. So I think it isn't as simple as that. I think Jesus might really be on *both* sides."

Dad didn't say anything. He frowned and tapped the ends of his fingers together. I could hear the boys upstairs, getting ready for bed. And Mom in the kitchen, talking on the phone.

"Like maybe He wanted Uncle T.T.'s crusade to do well, raise money, make people think about the bad things in Halloween, and all that, but He didn't want it to do so well that it would hurt other people. Because He cares about them, too. Brian says every good thing has a little bad, just like every bad thing has a little good.

"So if that's right, then maybe even a good thing like the crusade has to be controlled, to keep the bad in it from doing too much harm. And if there's even a tiny bit of good in a bad thing, a silver lining around a cloud, couldn't Jesus be on the side of that tiny bit of good? Even if Uncle T.T.'s on one side and I'm on the other, maybe Jesus could use both of us. And we could both win. Do you think that could be?"

"I'm not quite sure how to answer that," Dad said. "I can tell you what my father would have said. He would have said, just as T.T. does, that on this issue—on every one—Jesus would be on one side and the devil on the other. Period. Simple and clear.

"He was a good man, your grandfather, and a good preacher. He helped a lot of people." Dad cleared his throat and looked up at the light over the table. "But the truth is that he hurt some people too."

I'd seen pictures of my grandfather. He looked more like Dad than Uncle T.T., but very stern. In not one picture was he smiling.

"It may be true that there's a dark side to many good things. I've always thought that when the choices looked too simple, too clear cut, we needed to look a little closer. But if you're asking me to say that Jesus might work against something good and for something evil—no, I can't say that, Johnna."

"That isn't exactly what I meant." I was getting confused now. It had seemed clear when I started. "I don't know. I just know that working on the petition drive seemed to me to be the right thing to do. Do you mind that I did it? And that it got Halloween back in school?"

"I notice you didn't ask me before you did it."

"I was afraid you might say no." I swallowed around a sudden lump. "And I wasn't sure I could stop, even if you told me to."

Dad shook his head. "Somehow I am not surprised." Dad's face wasn't smiling, but I thought maybe his eyes were. "Better to keep it quiet than to disobey outright, eh? That's an interesting angle on 'Honor thy father.'"

"It felt safer, anyway."

Dad didn't say anything for a while. He just sat there, with a little frown on his face, staring off into space. Finally he looked at me again. "It may be, Johnna, that we honor our fathers best by being the person God meant us to be."

He shoved a pile of books out of the way and put a legal pad on the table in front of him. "'Honor thy father.' Sounds like a sermon topic to me."

Before I went to sleep that night, I thought about what Mom says all the time—"God works in mysterious ways." I still didn't know whether Jesus was on one side or the other or both. But I decided that no matter what they say, even grown-ups can't be absolutely *sure* they understand.

Chapter Sixteen

*I've been wondering what things will be like at school
after Halloween. Not the same, not even if Melissa
goes back to teasing me again. I've got some friends
now. Maybe not a best friend—Brian could almost
be, except it's too hard being best friends with a boy.
But Courtney Stubbins is going to our church now, so
maybe there's hope. And of course, I still have You.
At home or at school or anywhere, I always have You.*

Mrs. Teator was right. All the publicity about Halloween
brought so many people to our pageant that it sold out
every seat and we had to add two rows of folding chairs in
the back of the auditorium. Brian and I stood behind the
curtain as the audience was coming in, and (even though
it was absolutely against the rules) we peeked.

"Incredible!" Brian whispered. "Looks like half of
Bradyville is out there."

It was a big crowd, all right—it looked as big as the crusade. Brian's parents, with Sadie between them, were right in the middle of the front row. For some reason, when I saw them my eyes went blurry. Nobody from my family was out there. I closed the crack in the curtain. *You're here, though, aren't You?* It would have to be enough. "Places," I said. "We start in five minutes."

All through the show my hands shook so hard I could hardly turn the pages of the script, and even my ears perspired so that my earphones kept slipping. But I managed to call every single light change and sound cue exactly right. And just as Vanessa had promised, the theater magic worked. The bonfires looked and sounded like bonfires, the druid was weird and eerie, Samhain's voice echoed, and he moved in the swirling mist the smoke machine made so that he seemed to float.

Once, when Jamie was being pushed downstage, his robe got caught under the ladder wheel and everything lurched to a stop. I said a quick prayer as I imagined the whole thing toppling over. But Danny, underneath the ladder, jerked the robe loose, and probably no one in the audience even noticed because of the mist. The only other awful time was when Nicole's scream sent her into a coughing fit that wouldn't stop. She was probably the only human sacrifice in history who coughed the whole time she burned up.

At the end, when Jerome said "And we are still afraid" in his most druidy voice, the audience was real quiet, all the way through the closing of the curtains, and still when I gave the cue to open them again for the curtain call. But then they started to applaud, and pretty soon they were standing. After two curtain calls, the cast got Mrs. Teator out on stage and Melissa handed her a bouquet of flowers with a big sign that said, TWENTY-FIFTH ANNIVERSARY HALLOWEEN PROJECT. Then Mrs. Teator had all the crews come out from backstage and take a bow too. I went on and off again fast, so I could give the cue to close the curtains the last time.

"We did it!" Lashonda hollered a few minutes later, while everybody was still hugging each other and jumping up and down. "The ticket money's all counted, and we did it. Counting tickets and donations and orders for the videotape, we made the most money for UNICEF ever!"

For what seemed like five minutes, we kept up our "We are the sixth grade!" cheer.

At the Halloween prayer service the next night, the church was full. Courtney and her family came, and she sat down front with me and Mrs. Quigley. After Dad's invocation and a hymn, he introduced Uncle T.T. "It looks like my brother has done it again—where he goes, crowds follow. We thank you all for being here tonight, and hope you'll join us permanently, even when T.T. returns to his home territory next week and things calm down. He's off to search out the devil wherever he may be hiding, a task he has committed his life to accomplishing. If I were the devil, I'd be looking over my shoulder tonight, because T.T. Filkins is not going to give up or shut up."

"Your uncle's a fine preacher," Mrs. Quigley whispered, "and real flashy. But your father's a keeper."

Uncle T.T. came to the pulpit, as spectacular as ever in his white suit. His hair was falling over his forehead, and those blue eyes seemed to flash. "Right you are, James. I am not going to give up or shut up. We have a lot to be proud of and grateful for tonight. We have gathered God's people and we have changed the face of Halloween in Bradyville."

Courtney stuck her elbow in my side and I poked her back. There was one change that had come and then gone again.

"As Bradyville children trick-or-treat tonight, there is a citizen's committee on patrol, watching over them, keeping things in order. We—you and I and our crusade—made that change. We made people stop and think, made them take notice of the harm they sometimes welcome into their lives, the dangers even the most ordinary traditions may bring with them. We have alerted them to the devil's wiles."

The citizen's committee was an idea the mayor had suggested because of all the fuss. Brian's father was on it.

"And we are here tonight to thank God for the help He has given us and for the courage to stand up for what we believe in. We are also here on this Halloween night to thank God for the guarantee of eternal life that lets us handle our fear of death."

He paused.

I'd been running my hand along the top of my hymnal as I listened, and I looked up. He was looking right at me. "Yes," he said, "death is still with us. And yes, we are still afraid. Because we are only human."

Had someone told him about the pageant?

"But in our fear, we Christians don't have to turn to rituals of magic and sorcery, to ghosts and spirits. Because we have a promise from a power greater than any other. Jesus lived and died to give us the good news that death is not the end."

I nodded.

"Each of us can fight the devil every day, knowing that with Jesus on our side it is a fight we will eventually win. How we do that is a choice each of us makes. All Jesus asks is that we make it. And when we come to die in this life, we will know that we are entering another. Death is always with us, but life is eternal. Let us pray."

I sat for a second, thinking about what he'd said.

163

Then I noticed Courtney's voice next to me and joined in. ". . . who art in Heaven, hallowed be thy name. . . "

Brian joined us for cider and doughnuts at our house after the service. His hair was combed and his face scrubbed, but I could see little bits of green makeup around his ears from the "mouldering druid" costume he'd worn trick-or-treating with Kyle and Jerome.

Mom and Dad and Uncle T.T. were on the couch that soon wouldn't have to be my bed anymore. Matthew had the big frayed easy chair, and Mark was on one arm of it. Luke had brought a chair from the kitchen. "Thanks for inviting me," Brian said, sitting down with me on the floor. Things were still tense between me and the rest of the family, and it felt even tenser with Brian there. But he acted as if visiting in our house was the most ordinary thing in the world.

"We thought we should meet the person Johnna's been spending so much time with lately," Dad said.

Brian took a doughnut from the plate on the coffee table. "We had fun working on the pageant. She's a good writer."

"And the petition drive," Uncle T.T. asked, "was that fun too?" I thought he was teasing, but I couldn't be sure.

"That's strange, you know. It was. Maybe even more fun than the pageant! Especially since we managed to do what we set out to do. My parents say that in one way we're all on the same side, your family and ours."

"The same side?" Matthew and Mark said together.

Brian nodded. "You know, politically. They say that we Jews are a minority in this town and you are too, so we should all try to be sure that everybody's rights are protected. That way you can be heard and so can we."

Uncle T.T. frowned, but then nodded. Mom poured cider into mugs and motioned for me to pass them out.

"Johnna says you're going back to Texas to start a new crusade," Brian said.

Uncle T.T. took a mug and nodded again.

"Do you know what your theme is, yet?" Luke asked.

"I didn't until this very evening. It came to me as I was speaking at the service just now, when I said there were dangers in even the most ordinary traditions. I thought, of course, of Christmas."

"Dangers in Christmas?" Matthew asked.

Uncle T.T. turned to me. "Get me some paper and something to write with, would you, Johnna?"

I got a pad and pencil from the dining room and brought it to him, then sat back down next to Brian. Hiding what he was doing with his left hand, Uncle T.T. wrote something, then folded the sheet of paper and tore it into five pieces. He moved the doughnuts aside and laid the five pieces of paper, each with a single letter on it, on the coffee table. The letters spelled out *S-A-N-T-A*.

"Santa. So?" Dad said.

"Now watch," T.T. said, and he scrambled the letters and rearranged them. When he was done, they spelled out *S-A-T-A-N*.

"Fantastic!" said Luke. "Santa. Satan. Fantastic!"

Dad just shook his head. "Incredible."

Uncle T.T. was still grinning. "It just came to me. In a blinding flash."

"And what will the rest of your message be?" Dad asked.

"You know, the usual—commercialism, mainly. Satan focusing people on getting instead of giving, making them forget the real meaning of Christ's birth. And the pagan origins of the midwinter festival, of course." He looked at Brian and me. "I suppose you'll want to write a pageant about the history of Christmas now."

We both shook our heads. "No thanks," said Brian. "I don't write."

"It's a good message," Uncle T.T. said. "It'll work."

"Who could doubt a blinding flash?" Dad said, and sipped his cider.

"Santa, Satan," Luke said. "Just brilliant. Hey, Uncle T.T., you need a helper with this crusade?"

"You have school," Mom reminded him.

"There's Christmas vacation," he said. "I could fly down!"

"Winter vacation," Brian corrected him.

Uncle T.T. gathered up the pieces of paper. "Not a bad idea, Luke. I could always use a helper. Especially one with the gift."

"Take Johnna, too, then," Brian said. "She has the Filkins gift."

I stuck my elbow in his side to shut him up.

"Maybe our original plan to raise four preachers didn't go as wrong as we thought," Mom said. Dad must have told her. "Matthew, Mark, Luke, and Johnna. It's a little different than we intended. But maybe not wrong." She looked at me over her cider mug. "If it's really a *preaching* gift and not something else."

"That reminds me, Johnna," Dad said. "Would you read the scripture lesson Sunday?"

I nearly choked. Read the scripture? Me? "Sure!"

"So, do you want to be a preacher?" Brian asked later, as he was getting ready to leave.

I shrugged. "I don't know. I never thought about it."

"Well—I bet if you wanted to be, you could." He started out the door and then stopped. "I've got a better idea. Why don't you run for political office? I'll be your campaign manager. We'd make a great team—you for the Christian vote, me for the Jewish vote. What do you say? Senator Filkins? Governor Filkins?"

"I know," I said, and laughed. "President Filkins."

"Why not?"

When I had the living room to myself, the couch all made into a bed, I knelt beside my pillow and closed my eyes.

Dear Father, Son, and Holy Ghost, this is a regular prayer. I don't know if I'd want to be a preacher. And I don't know if I'd want to be a senator, either, much less president. But if I do have the gift, You gave it to me. So I hope You'll help me figure out how to use it. I think Uncle T.T. was saying at the service tonight that there are different ways to fight the devil. Dad does it one way, Uncle T.T. does it another way. There must be others, too. I just have to find mine.

Dad asked me to read the scripture on Sunday—well, I guess You know that. Now there's a miracle! I know You're busy looking after the world, so I won't take up much more of Your time. Just one last thing. I'll never get to go trick-or-treating, but this year I really got to have Halloween. And so did everybody else. Thank You, thank You, and thank You. Amen.